Itty Bitty Tiny Tall Tales

True Stories that Never Happened and More

K. B. CHANDRA RAJ

ARCHWAY
PUBLISHING

Scripture taken from the King James Version of the Bible.

Archway Publishing books may be ordered through booksellers or by contacting:

Archway Publishing
1663 Liberty Drive
Bloomington, IN 47403
www.archwaypublishing.com
1 (888) 242-5904

ISBN: 978-1-4808-6895-3 (sc)
ISBN: 978-1-4808-6896-0 (e)

Library of Congress Control Number: 2018911370

Print information available on the last page.

Archway Publishing rev. date: 10/04/2018

This book is dedicated to our parents, my wife's and mine.

They loved us unconditionally.

"Doubt thou the stars are fire;
Doubt thou that the sun doth move;
Doubt truth to be a liar"
– Shakespeare

Doubt not our undying gratitude.

ACKNOWLEDGEMENTS

My profound salaams and sincere salutations to:

Maureen Armstrong, librarian, the Whitneyville Branch of the Hamden Public Library and her capable assistants Pat and Ryan.

Without your help this project would not have seen daylight.

To my friend Doug Hawthorne, who I coopted to be a collaborator in this project, my heartfelt thanks.

He gave my manuscript, to the immense relief of my wife Siva, expert tonsorial treatment making it presentable to the public.

"When I first immigrated, I felt so stupid all the time... writing became a safe haven for me, a place where I wasn't accented, or my face didn't determine how someone thought of me."

Jenny Zhang
(Author of "Sour Heart" in an interview with the Guardian)

In America I (the writer) have been judged not by the color of my skin or, thank heaven, by the content of my character but rather by the tone, twang and timbre of my "funny" accent.

Rat-a-tat-tat, I am shot down with the question - "Where are you from?"

CHITCHAT WITH THE READER

The bombardment was blowing the trenches and the buildings in the neighborhood to bits. My brother and I sweated bullets. Our parents prayed. From the all-alert to the all-clear siren we lay prostrate under the bed, lying on our bellies. It was a time when food was scarce, fear and leisure alone were in abundance. The Brits had bolted from Malaysia with their tails between their legs. They promised to come back and they sure did. Although we remained caught during the intervening four years in the Vise Grip of anguish and anxiety, which seemed never ending, we pressed on inexorably. We kept the faith.

For our parents it must have been the "worst of times" for at their age, their stage in life, they think years ahead and dread the unknown and the unpredictable; but my brother and I were young and "to be young was very heaven." Let our parents worry about *our* future.

Reflecting on these days a feeling of sadness grips me. Nothing unites a family more than common danger, a family drawn close by more than consanguinity or mere proximity, a union forged by hardship and fear palpable and present. The vegetables we grew in our backyard were our "daily bread." We will do well to listen to the happy child we once were. Caught up in the mundane world of deadlines and dead- ends, we often stifle it's cries but cannot silence it's ever-present voice. Pray, has it not been said, "Blessed are the children, for theirs is the kingdom of heaven"? And the poet William Wordsworth believes "Heaven lies about us in our infancy."

We grow old and gray and feeble, but the child we once were providentially continues to dwell within us as the happy inner child. How else can one explain the urge to write in this fashion.

My brother and I, lying on the wooden floor of a stand-alone house in the jungle in Malaysia, would beg for more. Our cousin, a dear and good one who is no more, in polished, crystal clear diction would rack her brain to remember more stories of yore. Hercules and the Aegean stables, Samson and Delilah, Androcles and the Lion, David and Goliath, and many, many more. For our cousin story telling was as natural and human as breathing. She took pleasure in it. She would not only relate a story, she would also explain the lesson we should learn from it. Every story she told served the purpose of illustrating a moral.

It would be germane at this point to inform the reader that during these tumultuous times there were no books because the Japs, the brutal occupying force who had the license to run amok unfettered, forbade the possession of English books. If caught owning one, you could, not metaphorically speaking but literally, "lose your head." Our dad returning from work would relate to us gruesome tales of defiant men's heads being chopped off and stuck on poles.

Even the mightiest, being human, our cousin would say, have flaws be they physical or of character. In Samson it was the hair. In Achilles it was the heel. In Hamlet it was vacillation. Remember: "To be or not to be." All humans have their "Achilles heel."

In Samuel Beckett's "Waiting for Godot" two characters, Vladimir and Estragon, wait endlessly for someone named Godot. Unfortunately, Vladimir and Estragon cannot agree where or when they are to meet with Godot. They do not have even the foggiest idea what Godot looks or sounds like. All they know is that they have to wait at a tree. They may be waiting still.

"Don't wait for things to happen," she said. "Make it happen."

Sisyphus for his self-aggrandizing and deceitful ways was condemned to an eternity of rolling a boulder uphill only to see it roll down again. What did Sisyphus do, asked our cousin rhetorically? "Of course, you don't know," she would say with an endearing smile. To the complete bewilderment and chagrin of the gods, Sisyphus, whistling perhaps

"Don't Worry-Be Happy," enjoyed rolling the boulder up and then seeing the boulder roll down. He was having fun.

"Whatever tedious chore you are assigned, see some fun in doing it."

"Do you know how Hercules cleaned the Aegean stables? No? I'll tell you."

King Augeas owned more cattle than anyone in Greece. He had many herds of cows, bulls, goats, sheep and horses. Every night the cowherds and the goatherds drove thousands of animals to the stables. You can well imagine the condition the stables were in.

When Hercules was approached by the king and asked whether he could clean the stables, his prompt response was, "No problem." In Greek, of course. He cleaned the awful mess in a single day and this is how he did it.

First Hercules tore a big opening in the wall of the cattle yard where the stables were. Then he made another opening in the wall on the opposite side of the yard. Next he dug wide trenches to two rivers which flowed nearby. Hercules turned the course of the rivers into the yard. The rivers gushed through the stables, flushing them out, and the mess flowed out the hole in the wall on the other side of the wall.

Done!

It may have been a "Herculean task" for ordinary folks but not for Hercules.

"Anything can be done if you set your mind to it. You, too, can be a Hercules."

It was not known at the time that Hercules consumed large amounts of the energy drink "Red Bull," coupled with regular workouts at the gym.

King Shahryar caught his wife making love with a servant.

"I will not spend another night alone," he swore. He married a woman one day and put her to death the following day.

At the end of three years and over one thousand brides executed, the kingdom had now run out of virgins while the sexual appetite of the king continued crying out loud for more.

There was panic for the last virgin standing was Shahrazad, the only daughter of the King's "Chief of Staff."

Shahrazad's father was distraught. But Shahrazad was confident. Saying "don't worry daddy, I'll handle him," she readily agreed to take on the king, while the subjects held their collective breath.

On the wedding night Shahrazad begins to tell the king a tantalizing tale but shrewdly does not end it. The king, eager to know how it ends, postpones the execution. This goes on for one thousand and one nights.

The following is the unexpurgated version of what actually took place.

At this point while lying in bed (he would always listen to the stories in bed in a reclining position with his minions fanning him), the king sends word to all the ministers and chiefs to assemble in the ornate Grand Hall along with Shahrazad. There was trepidation throughout the kingdom as to the fate of their much loved Shahrazad. When all had assembled in the great hall, the king in full regalia walked up to Shahrazad and, removing one of the rings he had on and falling on his knees, uttered the following words:

"I love you with all my heart. I cannot imagine my life without you in it. I hope you will say 'yes' and make me the happiest man alive."

Many wonder today whether this was a harbinger of the Meghan Markle and Prince Harry romance and subsequent betrothal that will follow centuries later.

Our cousin kept us enthralled not for one thousand and one nights but for four sepulchral years. These stories transported us from the dread of imminent danger--what with the sound of British B-20 bombers overhead--to a world of stories wherein we found safe harbor.

On reflection it would appear not much has changed from "Arabian Nights" to "Trumpian Days." The insatiable appetite, I mean.

Oedipus accidentally kills his father and marries his mother. When the truth of their relationship became known, Oedipus's wife who was also his mother hanged herself. This haunting, never to be forgotten, tragedy is communicated to us through the medium of a story.

There are some truths best communicated by stories. About one hundred years ago, while a man was leisurely scanning the morning paper, he was jolted out of his skin to read his name in the obituary column. The newspaper had by mistake reported the death of the wrong person. His first response was shock.

When he regained his composure, his second thought, understandably, was to find out what people had said about him. The obituary read "Dynamite king dies," and there were reports such as "The merchant of death is no more." The man was the inventor of dynamite, and when he read the words "merchant of death," he felt miserable. He asked himself the question, "Is this how I am going to be remembered?"

From that day on he began working for peace. His name was Alfred Nobel. He is remembered today because of the much sought after Nobel Prize.

Mothers with sweet plaintive voices rock their little ones to sweet slumber by telling them tiny stories before kissing them good night. Restive babies, strapped in their bouncy seats, are bamboozled to eat a few more morsels of food by stories, stories that never become dull even after many repetitions.

"*The shoe maker, a kindly old man, had an urgent delivery the next day,*" says the mother to the petulant child. "*But he was very tired. He fell asleep at the work bench. As soon as it was midnight, there came two little elves. They sat upon the shoemaker's bench, took up the unfinished work that was cut out, and began to ply their little fingers. They stitched and rapped and tapped at such a rate that it was all done when the shoemaker woke up.*"

What are lullabies but short, very short, stories sweetened by rhyme. The mother croons "Twinkle, twinkle little star . . .," and a vocal intimacy between mother and child that will endure a lifetime is born.

Alexander the Great was eager to hear stories at night in the company of his friends and associates. He had under his pillow, alongside his dagger, a copy of the "Iliad."

Lincoln before issuing the Emancipation Declaration, a hallowed moment in history, informed all the members of the cabinet in attendance that humorist Artimus Ward had sent him his book. He read aloud to all present a chapter which everyone thought was very funny. The chapter he read was "Highhanded Outrage at Utica."

Geoffrey Chaucer wrote the Canterbury Tales almost six hundred years ago. He wrote in rhyme, the style of the time. The language, Middle English as we now know it, may be strange but the people he wrote about are no different from modern folks--the same thoughts and motives, the greed for money, for love and the desire to be happy and entertained. These do not change. This is the reason for its popularity.

Stories are told to pass the time.

In the Canterbury Tales the pilgrims plan to travel from Southwark to Canterbury, a distance of about sixty miles. In those leisurely days it would take them four days by horse. To pass the time in a clubby, convivial atmosphere they agree that each of the pilgrims will tell four stories, two on the way to the shrine and two on the way back.

Don't we all want to know what women desire most. The answer can be found in the Canterbury Tales ("The Wife of Bath's Tale").

A knight in the court of King Arthur had fallen afoul of the king and the king said he must die. The Queen begged for the king's mercy, and the knight was therefore handed over to the Queen for whatever action she deemed fitting.

"Sir Knight," the Queen said. "It's up to you to save your neck from the ax. You must tell me the one thing that women desire most." The knight is given a year and a day to return with the answer. The knight travels far and wide, and at the end of the allotted time he brings the Queen the right answer and thus saves his neck. Who would not want to know what the correct answer is?

In the present age of television, telephone, texting, 280-character tweeting and drive–throughs, there is neither the time nor the appetite for the <u>Iliad</u>, <u>Ulysses</u>, or <u>War and Peace</u>. (It took me several weeks to finally put away "Moby Dick.") Reading <u>War and Peace</u>, I have heard it said, is like driving across Texas – "exhausting," to put it kindly.

Short stories have come to fill the void. With his "Twice Told Tales" Nathaniel Hawthorne (1804-1864) is considered the beginning of the English language short story, a claim hotly contested by admirers of Washington Irving (1783-1859). Irving's hysterically funny Rip Van Winkle, who would "rather starve on a penny than work for a pound," while away from his termagant wife and after hearty gulps from his hip flask, takes a "cat nap" in the Catskill Mountains and wakes up twenty years later completely in the dark that the American Revolution had passed by him.

Short stories will always continue to be popular. They provide a rapid medium of entertainment, and what is more they do not require a protracted attention span and the strain on our memory is miniscule. In a brief period, one can listen to or read a short story and feel entertained.

Duncan Dieterly likens a short story to the final stages of a bull fight wherein the "matador brings the bull in closer and closer and finally sets the sword for the kill." We should not be misled into believing writing a short story is "as easy as pie." Again, from Duncan Dieterly, the "Independent Writing and Editing Professional":

> In a sense it is harder to write a solid short story than a longer work of fiction since time is the essence and words must be used with precision and profundity. While it may take less time to weave or relate a short story, it is far harder to realize the anticipated outcome using this briefer form.

A short story should have four basic attributes: it should tell a story, it should be sufficiently entertaining to hold the reader's attention, it should be thought provoking, and ideally it should evoke an emotional response.

Surprisingly not many, even avid, readers are familiar with the genre, "Flash Fiction", a fictional work of extreme brevity. It's also known as Micro Fiction, Minute Story, Pocket Size Story, Palm Size Story, Sudden Fiction, The Dribble, and in China Wei Xing Xiao Shuo.

The most original descriptions of Flash Fiction, in my opinion, are "Smoke-Long Story" and "Cigarette-Long Story," stories which promise to let the readers relish the sights and sounds of an entire make-believe world before he or she has time to finish one delicious cigarette.

Like Aesop's Fables in the West and the Panchatantra and Jataka Tales in India, they possess the ability to hint at a larger story to the fertile mind. To an enterprising writer a few lines are sufficient to trigger a short story:

John meets Debbie's father. Prefers him.

The date went poorly. Wendall and Marge discovered they had nothing in common and didn't know what to talk about when they woke up in the morning.

Tony waited on the school steps for his mom to pick him up. She never came, wanting him to be more independent now that he has been made principal of the school.

Jack climbed once and got gold coins. He climbed again and got the hen that laid golden eggs. He climbed again and got the harp that sings on its own.

And when Jack climbed once more, the bean stalk prayed, "Please God, Not Again."

The moving last words of Pancho Villa, the Mexican Revolutionary general: "Don't let it end like this, tell them I said something."

Over the years short stories have grown to be very popular and have now come to stay. Campers around fires spin out short stories; buddies at the bar over a beer ("Did you hear this one about Billy Bush and Trump?") swap smutty short stories and when they get home tell a different story. We all tell each other stories. That's one of the ways we exist, one of the ways we know we're alive and well.

Haven't we all heard at a gathering of friends, if someone in their midst relates an event of questionable probity, someone else will likely intercede with the remark, "Don't mind him, that's his 'short story'." "Short story" here is a polite shorthand for "fib."

Short stories engage the reader immediately, and in a few pages the reader experiences the suspense and thrill of, say, watching a tight rope walker without a safety net. Many readers have come to love the short story because of the small number of characters, often not more than three or four, the easy narrative voice, and, of course, the swift surprise endings. One of the most resilient forms of entertainment, the short story with its delicately controlled pace, timing, and sheer wonderment has come to provide us a welcome distraction in a world sadly suffuse with internecine wars, hatred, prejudice, murder and mayhem. It's a much sought-after special treat like a chocolate bar (with nuts) to be savored and enjoyed swiftly in one delicious, scrumptious session.

In the book you hold in your hands, you will be reading "*Tiny Tall Tales*" with an unexpected twist to pique your curiosity and prod you to continue reading. Do not be put off that they are just short stories. Less can be more; an admirer's subtle, stolen sidelong glance more consequential than the long look or stare.

Aren't parables and anecdotes short stories that teach us a moral in an amusing way, meant for all of humanity irrespective of their religious beliefs, culture, race, color, or age?

The short story's colossal power results from its brevity and restraint. "Brevity is the soul of wit," said the Bard. Remember James Madison who wrote the first drafts of the U.S. Constitution and Mahatma Gandhi who drove the British out of India were all in height only five-foot-four. There was so much packed into so little. Consider how difficult it must be to paint a landscape on a grain of rice. And it has been done. Aren't we all enthralled by the suspense endings of O. Henry, the bizarre situations of the Sherlock Holmes adventures, the creepy nightmares of Edgar Allan Poe, and the quirky humor of Damon Runyon? Earnest Hemingway, Mark Twain, Rabindranath Tagore and Truman Capote were giant short story tellers, builders of narratives, tellers of concise tales. In their hands the short story, a compaction of plot, character, mood, and structure, becomes one of the most artful of literary forms.

Consider this story, purported to be the world's shortest horror story:

> The last man on earth sat alone in a room. There was a
> knock at the door.

Guy De Maupassant states the author's aim is not to tell a story to amuse us or to appeal to our feelings but to compel us to *reflect and to understand the occult and deeper meaning of events.*

Stodgy! Very stodgy!

No, dear reader, these itty bitty tiny tall tales are meant to amuse you, to help you pass the time with a smile while you wait to be called to the dentist's chair; they are to be read at Starbucks (after having paid for a cup) while you are waiting for your partner to join you, or at the gym to keep you engaged while sweating it out on the tread mill.

"I read for pleasure and that is the moment at which I learn the most," says Margaret Atwood. Well said!

1

The Sum of Our Parts

"Ivanka will be the president's eyes and ears." (News Report)

Once a year body parts hold a convention. On this day they exchange compliments and trade insults freely.

The meeting is called to order.

"Why do these humans have to always bring us into their conversation?" asked the Head.

"What do you mean?" asked Feet.

"They always want to get a 'head start.' When he is in love, it has to be 'head over heels.' If he flunks the math test, then he does not have a 'head' for numbers."

"Now - Now" said Feet. "You do not have to put your nose into this, you nosey thing. This is why humans say "I cannot get my head around this or that, you dummy."

"I feel so privileged," said Hands. "My thanks go out to humans when they bring their palms together in prayer and shake hands when they greet and depart. When he does well it's 'thumbs up and two thumbs up' and never forget, folks, that 'the hand that rocks the cradle rules the world.'"

"Now who's talking?" said Mouth addressing Hands. "The journey of a thousand miles starts not with hands, you oaf, but with a single step; and when the journey is completed, how wonderful you feel when you put both your feet up. You cannot even scratch your own back. You have to go around begging. You scratch my back and I'll scratch yours. Why don't you stay where you are and continue to twiddle your thumb?"

"Aw! When you take an oath, you do not put your mouth on the bible. You place your hand. I feel so privileged when that happens."

"Now we know why."

"Know what why?"

"There are two hands, two ears, two feet and only one mouth. Thank God only one mouth and that too is one too many. You are just a mouthpiece. I do not have the stomach for family squabbles. So, shut up."

"Even Shakespeare is guilty" said Ears.

"Shakespeare? How come?"

"Did he not say, 'Friends, Romans, Countrymen, lend me your ears?' How can we be so sure he will return them?"

Then they heard from down below the pair whimpering, "How low can human beings go?" and they saw the pair shedding tears. "Why do humans have to say only of men 'He does not have the balls'? That's gender discrimination!"

"Could you all please do me a big favor? I'll forever be grateful." A sorrowful plea was heard from the far end.

Everyone turned around.

"Now what do you want?" they all asked.

"Stop calling me asshole."

"All right. Then we will call you 'shit hole.' It has the presidential imprimatur."

The meeting is adjourned

2

In Silence Please

Anthony had been widowed for 40 years. I have known him for many years. Once when I asked him whether a second marriage did not interest him, with a far- off look in his eyes he shook his head from left to right. I never broached the topic again. His only child died some time ago in a car accident. He lives alone. He walks with a limp and a cane. On days of inclement weather Anthony does not open his shop. He likes to talk and is forever abuzz with questions.

Some nondescript pictures adorned the wall, and the furniture is time worn and weather beaten. The serene snip, snip, snip of his scissors is the only sound that breaks the genteel silence at this Barber Shop. There have been days when he has dropping scissor, comb and all and made a dash for the bathroom saying, "It's the water pill I'm taking for pressure. I'll be back."

Today, the weather being pleasant, he opened his shop around 8.30 in the morning and was waiting more for company than for customers.

It was 11.30 A.M. He had finished reading the New Haven Register, and around 11.40 in walks the first customer, a first timer. Anthony is delighted. There'll be a lot to talk about.

Anthony receives customer Exxe graciously and leads him to the chair and drapes him with the cape. Customer removes his glasses and places them on the table in front.

Anthony decides it's time to talk.

He asks, "How would you like to have your hair cut, sir?"

Exxe gives him a steely stare through the mirror in front of him and replies:

"IN SILENCE PLEASE"

Anthony passed away two years ago.

3

Cash for Trash

It was going to be a mammoth celebration; celebrating for wildly exceeding forecast. Representatives from all over the world were gathering to honor him at the Waldorf Hotel. He was grandly dressed and excitedly pacing up and down the corridor. He did not want to be late. She was beautifying herself endlessly. She had bought an expensive dress for the occasion.

He wanted this day to go without errors. To save time he went over to the garage and drove his Porsche to the porch and kept it purring. Finally, she emerged radiant and beaming. She sashayed into the car and they left.

On the Merrit Parkway in Stamford cars were crawling. "Must be some road work," he muttered somewhat annoyed. She took the opportunity to check in the mirror to see how she looked. Just the way she wanted to present herself. She put away the hand bag and idly looked out. Her eyes traveled a little to the left and espies a woman who looks familiar. Very familiar.

"Stop! Stop!" she yelled. "Pull over. To the shoulder. Soon"

"What on earth has got into you?"

He pulled over and parked on the shoulder.

She ran down to level ground.

"What are you doing, Ma?"

"I am collecting empty bottles and cans to exchange for cash. Oh! You look so pretty, darling. I am so proud of you."

4

Revenge Sweet and Sour

On the day he was born, the father walked out of the house and never returned. He was a gambler, big time. The son saw with pity and horror the hardship the mother went through working several jobs, saving every penny for food and board.

"I'll hunt him down and kill him Ma" the son swore.

"Never do that, son, if you love me. He is a good man. His only weakness was gambling. Perhaps he lost all his money. That's why he left."

"I'll kill him, Ma! I'll kill him!"

He bought a gun and carried an old I.D. photo of his father, which he had enlarged, and set out in search. He went to Reno, Las Vegas, Paris, Singapore, Monte Carlo, London, the gambling capitals of the world. He spent several days visiting the casinos and showed his father's picture and inquired whether any- one had seen him as he had an urgent message for him.

"Sorry, no" they all said.

He was despondent. He always wanted to visit Gibraltar. In Gibraltar, he visited the casino. "Just in case he turns up here," he thought. He went over to the manager and showed him the picture.

"Yes, a gentleman like the one in the picture comes in here every Wednesday sharp at nine o'clock. Could be him," he said.

On Wednesday, the son, with the gun loaded, sat in the Casino facing the entrance. Minutes seemed hours. Close to nine o'clock he got nervous. He began to sweat.

"I must kill him, I must," he swore.

Nine o'clock sharp a gentleman walked through the front entrance all smiles and waving to all. He knew it must be him. He felt it in his gut, an instant vicarious connection that could not be mistaken. His heart began to beat faster and faster.

He pulled out the gun, attached the silencer and took aim.

His hands went limb. He just could not do it. Kill his father.

5

Blind Love

Johnny was very much in love with her but could never summon sufficient courage to tell her. His salivary glands would go dry even if he only just glanced at her. There would be profuse secretion of the sweat glands each time he spoke to her. His blood pressure would take wild swings even if by mistake he brushed against her. Because of her he suffered from nausea, blurred vision, and weak knees. This surging love kept him awake for a good part of the night. He kept a close tab on her and was intimately aware of all her movements. He knew the drive to her house. He knew the trees he would pass, the fire hydrants, the dogs barking behind their fences.

He managed to find out when her birth day was and on that day visited her with a bouquet of large red roses. Nervously he handed her the roses.

When Caroline saw the red roses, her face changed crimson. She screwed her face and put them away. Johnny was very disappointed. Did not understand why she was upset. Is it because my note said "lovingly," he wondered. The Romeo in him that was in full bloom shrank to a bud and so Johnny walked away with a heavy heart and a perplexed head, unable to make any sense of it at all.

As soon as Johnny left, she screamed, "Doesn't he know mommy was wearing red when she died in the car accident? I hate red!"

Ten years later Caroline attended Johnny's funeral. He died in a car accident running the red light. He was color blind.

Johnny did not know that in life it is not good to want a thing too much, as was his love for Caroline. It sometimes chases the luck away. You must want it just enough - not more, not less. And what is more you must be tactful not to offend the gods of karma.

6

The Silver Lining

Eve always longed to be financially independent. For too long she had been dependent on the munificence of her husband. The children had finished college and have left home. It was about time she made some money that she will spend "foolishly" according to the dictates of her fancy.

To raise additional capital for her jewelry designing business she had traded in her year- old car for an older one advertised to be in "mint condition."

It was winter and it was dark when she set out to keep an appointment with a client. The old car began huffing and puffing and after several turns to circumvent road blocks the beast in "mint condition" ground to a halt. She was not quite sure where on earth she had landed. It was down town somewhere in the New Haven vicinity. She got out of the car and looked around. The shops were all closed. She could see one place with the lights on. The neon lights blinked, "Drink and Dance till Dawn"

As she had no cell phone she decided to walk up to what she fancied to be a night club. There she accosted a large man, his stomach lazing over his waist band, who sprawled over the counter with a cigarette dangling from his mouth.

"May I use your phone, sir?"

The man, sweeping her from top to toe with his lascivious eyes, replied, "Five dollars please."

"I didn't ask to buy the phone, sir, just to use it."

"Lady, let's call it "corkage." Take it or beat it. I'm in no mood for an argument."

She took a ten- dollar bill and handed it to him.

He pocketed the ten dollars. "Thanks for the tip."

From where she stood she could see a gentleman on the phone leaning against the wall in loud conversation. He did not appear to be in any hurry.

She moved closer to the gentleman on the phone so that she could grab the phone as soon as he finished. From her new position, she could see the stage in diffused lighting. What she saw was disgusting.

A woman, a "Stormy Daniels" look-alike, save for the "sacred" parts partially covered, plain flesh in the raw. She slithered sensuously around a tarnished brass pole pulling a feather boa between her thighs and around her body. She then bent over in different suggestive positions and the patrons were cheering, clapping, whooping, slinging obscenities and throwing five- dollar bills. She sat on the laps of patrons of her choosing and nibbled at their ears.

Eve's disgust now turned to curiosity. She began watching very closely the various moves. Disgust that turned to curiosity now blossomed to fascination.

The telephone was free. She called her husband and waited outside the club.

"Sorry Babe. I was down in the basement and took some time to get to the phone."

"Are you O.K," Tony asked.

She sighed and leaned over and gave him a full- blooded kiss.

"I am now. I learned a lot from the whole experience."

"What was that, sweetie?"

Blushing broadly, Eve replied, "I'll show you when we get home honey. You're going to like it."

"And this our life, exempt from public haunt, finds tongues in trees, books in running brooks, sermons in stones, and good in everything. I would not change it."

William Shakespeare: "As You Like It"

7

Honesty (not) Always the Best Policy

Piyadasa felt very lonely living in a small town in Norway. He was the only Sri Lankan and was hankering for the company of a compatriot with whom he could communicate in Sinhala, his mother tongue. At the mall, seated sipping tea in a kiosk, he saw a young man at the far end who he was certain was a Sri Lankan.

Piyadasa went up to him and they spoke. He was a Sri Lankan. His name was Somadasa. He lived in the neighboring town. They were both bachelors.

Friday nights they would spend in each other's apartment, cook and sleep over. They became very close friends. While Piyadasa was keen on marrying a Sri Lankan, Somadasa was not particular. Their passion was cricket. Piyadasa played for Richmond College in Galle and Somadasa for St. Peter's College in Colombo, though not contemporaneously.

After two years of intimate friendship Somadasa confided to Piyadasa.

"Machan, I must confess. My name is Somasundram. My parents both doctors, had no time for me and I was brought up by an Ayah."

"I went to Jaffna and joined the Tiger separatist movement. It was I who planned the Central Bank bombing. I was horrified by the carnage and became disgusted and disillusioned by the movement. I abandoned it."

"It was not safe living in Sri Lanka. The 'Tigers' were out to get me. So, I changed my name and here I am. I hope you understand."

"You have changed. That's good. It does not matter anymore," responded Piyadasa.

Later Somadasa left several messages on Piyadasa's answering machine and none of them were returned.

What Somadasa did not know—could not know—is that Piyadasa's niece, accompanying her father to the Central Bank in Colombo, died in the bomb blast.

8

Dim & Dum: The power of indolence

"Consider the lilies of the field, how they grow: they toil not, neither do they spin." [Mathew 6:28, KJV]

Dim and Dum collected their coffee from the nymphet at their habitual rendezvous and proceeded to their usual corner.

Dim: You were all praise for indolence. How come?

Dum: My wife keeps telling me "Get a job, get a job"

Dim: What's wrong with that?

Dum: I'll tell you what's wrong. It's a lot of hooey.

What was Adam but a loafer in search of a woman to spend time with? He was not bothered by the gyrations of the stock market. He was happy so long as there were sufficient apples.

Newton's discovery, remember? – There he was snoozing under an apple tree one sunny day, when an over ripe fruit detached itself from the branch and fell on his head – and the law of gravity was born.

You must have heard of Diogenes, haven't you?

Dim: Of course the man who propounded the philosophy of cynicism.

Dum: Bull shit, man. Sleeping wherever he chose and begging for food, he spent all his time carrying a lamp during the day saying he was looking for an honest man.

And when any one mentions the name Archimedes all that comes to your mind is a man bustling past people naked and dripping shouting "Eureka, Eureka," I have found it.

You have heard of the Buddha, haven't you?

Dim: They refer to him as Lord Buddha.

Dum: Yah, yah. All day he sat smiling under the Bo tree with a bowl collecting alms. When a passer-by asked him "what are you doing man – why don't you get a job", he replied, "I am meditating." Now we all know why he was putting on weight.

You have heard of Gandhi, haven't you?

Dim: They refer to him as Mahatma Gandhi. Now what have you against him?

Dum: He did no work. He did worse. He stopped others from working. He and his followers slept across rail tracks and prevented law abiding people from going to work.

John the Baptist became a saint only because he was beheaded. Peter outdid John the Baptist. He demanded he be crucified upside down.

Dim: Jesus!

Dum: Did you say Jesus? I'll tell you about him. He and his bachelor buddies in Nike sandals went all around talking shop. That's what they did.

Dim: Have you anything more against Jesus?

Dum: Of course.

Dim: Like what?

Dum: He encouraged party drinking by turning water into wine. He was a spoil sport with a short temper.

Dim: What do you mean?

Dum: When a few guys were playing chess, he turned the tables on them.

Dim: Never forget. Jesus raised Lazarus from the dead.

Dum: You really believe in that B.S.?

Dim: Of course, I do.

This is what happened. Jesus whispered into the ear of Lazarus, "You've won the mega power ball." And he jumped up.

Dim: Oh my God.

Dum: God did you say? I'll tell you about him too. He worked for six days and then called it a day. Since then either he's on paid sick leave or on workmen's comp.

Dim gets up and leaves.

Dum: Don't leave. I have more. This God you worship allowed his son to be nailed to the cross. What parent will do that? He was so vain he prodded Isaac to sacrifice his son. Fortunately, at the last minute he changed his mind.

Dum: How on earth can anyone justify collective punishment?

Dim: Collective punishment? What on earth are you talking about?

Dum: Do you know how many innocent men, women and children were killed in Sodom and Gomorrah? I suppose you will say it was collateral damage like bombing I.S.I.S. targets.

Dum: Where are you going?

Dim: I have had enough. I'm going to get a bowl and sit under a Bo tree.

Dum with the satisfied smirk of Lucifer whispers sotto voce, "There's one more disciple in the bag."

Trees reach great heights without even trying.

9

Bingo

Auditory hallucinations; Inner speech; Interior monologue; back and forth conversation; it all happens in my brain . . . or so I think. Night and day. The voices have accent and pitch. They are very private and are audible only to me. So I think. Believe me, they sound like real people. To state it plainly, I hear voices. This has been going on for some time. I am worried.

Before I leave home I peep out the window. Is it going to rain? Should I take my trench coat with me? Ah, it's such a bother, I think, and so I leave the coat behind even though the voice keeps telling me, "Take the trench coat." If it rains and I get wet, the voice makes a big noise in my ears, "I told you so, I told you so."

Since this voice has become so much part of my life, I give it a name and call him/her "Bingo." I have no idea whether Bingo is male or female.

Throughout the day and at night too, Bingo is talking to me. As I approach a traffic light turning yellow, Bingo will start talking to me. "Slow down, slow down," and I very often will step on the gas and just make it by a couple of feet. I then wait for Bingo to speak. "Believe me, one day you are going to regret not heeding my warning."

In the night while I am asleep, Bingo will wake me up, "Time to urinate, up, up, up," Bingo will say. I plead, "A little more time Bingo, please." Bingo will not talk. Bingo will make me so uneasy I have to obey. From the bed to the bathroom I go.

On very rare occasions Bingo leaves me alone like when watching "Saturday Night Live." These occasions are fleeting and very few.

I have given this, I call it ailment, a great deal of thought. About Bingo's control over me. Maybe I should see a shrink. Just then Bingo will intercede. "It will cost you a lot of money you don't have and all for nothing because you will not be able to get rid of me. Your friends are bound to know you saw a shrink. After that they will treat you like you are crazy. They will stare at you searching for symptoms. They will discuss you behind your back." At times such as this, when thinking of what I should do, I freeze on the spot, mindless of what I may be doing or wherever I may be. So much so I've been asked, "Are you O.K?"

Anyway, going to see a shrink is a lot of work. I will be passed from doctor to doctor like a baton in a relay. At the end of it all how will I ever know I have been cured.

One day I decided I cannot take this anymore. I decided to silence Bingo once and for all. But I could not figure out how to do that without hurting myself. So, I gave up the idea.

May be the answer is not to try to get rid of Bingo. What cannot be cured, the sages say, must be endured. My mother used to say that if you cannot beat them, join them.

So, I tell myself to learn to live with Bingo. Appreciate the good things Bingo does for me. For example, Bingo wakes me up in the night to urinate so I don't wet the bed

There are times Bingo has fun at my expense. For instance, while driving, Bingo may order me to turn left when it turns out later I clearly should have turned right. When I am in distress, I can hear him laughing.

I have often wondered why Bingo can't be of help. Why can't he tell me where I left my car keys, my spectacles and the socks, the missing single? Why doesn't Bingo go over to President Trump and get in the way of his compulsive tweeting? That would be yeoman service. No. I do not always get answers to my pleas.

There are certain chores I alone have to do. That's Bingo's message.

I have thrown in the towel. I am going to listen to Bingo. Come to think of it, Bingo says the right things. Ah! Ah! Ah! You don't need that extra helping. No! No! No! No more chips. You've had enough. Bingo has prevented me from taking imprudent, impulsive actions.

Friends! Listen to your Bingo.

Bingo! You are the Boss. You tame the inner beast in me.

10

Life's Sweepstakes

Daphne called her mother and cried, "With his new job as Director of Sales Harry is seldom home. I fear he has another woman. Please Ma, tell dad to do something. I cannot take it anymore. What with two kids and all."

Mom got on to the father. "Do something, John. The poor girl is in distress."

And so dad John decided to visit the daughter and learn for himself. It transpired Harry, claiming he has to visit the company branches, was rarely at home. On Fridays, claiming he has one thing or another, he comes home very late or not at all. John also surmised Harry's romantic ardor had cooled off.

He said to the daughter, "Give me a few days, darling, and I'll come up with something."

Daddy John hired a gum shoe to shadow his son-in-law, and the detective reported that Harry was living with another woman in the next town.

After a talk with his very close childhood buddy Charlie, John put his plan into operation. He began visiting the local bar and made careful note of the regulars. One stood out as attractive and flirty. One night he accosted her in the bar and proposed his plan for which Rita was to receive two hundred dollars.

The next Friday John handed over the money and dropped Rita

within walking distance of Harry's "other" house. Rita barged into the house, and there was Harry with a woman making love on the sofa with the television full blast. Rita began yelling at Harry, "How many women do you need, Harry. You seem to be changing women more often than you do your underwear."

"Excuse me miss, but you are not his first and will not be his last. He will dump you as he did all the other women." The woman on the sofa began yelling and screaming and throwing things at Harry and kicked both of them out.

Once out Harry asked Rita, "Who the hell are you?"

Rita replied, "Get back to your wife, you silly. You will thank me for it."

Harry went back home. Neither he nor his father-in-law spoke a word of what had taken place.

Daughter Daphne began to observe that daddy was in no hurry to return home to mummy. He was spending most of the time in the bar with Rita. They were now madly in love. John decided to leave his wife for Rita, but someone had to break the news to his wife, Daphne's mom.

Who else, John figured, than his and his wife's mutual childhood buddy Charlie?

John disclosed to Charlie that he is leaving his wife for Rita.

"Could you please break this to Evelyn? You are the only one I can ask for such a big favor. Please do it for me."

After much pleading and persuasion Charlie agreed.

"Charlie!" John begged. "Be gentle. Comfort her. I don't want her hurt too much."

Charlie promised to do his best.

Charlie went directly to Evelyn and conveyed the news.

Evelyn took it calmly. "So we don't have to meet secretly, eh Charlie? How about a beer?"

11

Silent Treatment

Ustinov brought her from Vietnam when the war was over. He married her in the United States. She was young, coy and could speak just a few words of English. In fact, she spoke very little. She had no friends. Ustinov called her Lily because she was pretty and frail. Lily attended to all of Ustinov's needs. Cooked, washed and pressed clothes and attended hand and foot on Ustinov. She would not eat until Ustinov had had his meal. She made sure all his needs were met.

Ustinov often took off with his friends for days leaving Lily alone. When he came home, she would be there attending to some household chore. One time Ustinov came home from his outing with his pals a week earlier than planned. When Ustinov arrived home, Lily was not there. She appeared the day before he was to have returned.

Ustinov did not ask any questions. Neither did Lily offer an explanation. Since that day, Ustinov stopped gallivanting about with his friends. The two of them did things together. They lived happily ever after.

12

Better Luck Next Time

On the second day of his honeymoon they arrested him and put him in the clink, and there he remained for ten years. On the day of his release friends and relatives were present to welcome him. His wife, ten years later, prettier than ever, was thrilled to take him home.

After the party was over and all have gone, there were four children trailing behind his wife.

"So, these must be the neighbor's children, I guess," he said.

"No, they are all mine," she said. She pointed to the first, Arthur. "You see, I could not manage to do all the garden work. Arthur's dad was of great help."

"That one is Sam. The children were constantly falling ill, and I had to call the pediatrician to the house many times. He is a good man. He was very helpful."

"The third one over there is Victor. I used to get very depressed in my constant loneliness and Father Ignatius would drop by at all hours to cheer me up."

"That little brat under the sofa is a puzzle. At times I feel he resembles the mail man, at others the U.P.S. guy."

She sidled up and kissed him, saying, "Don't cry, darling, the next one will be just yours and mine. I promise. What a pity the first day of our honeymoon was wasted because of my bashfulness."

13

On My Way Home

During winter, I leave the library before it gets dark. I can be home in ten minutes. Today my friend Bill held me up. It was dark when I set out for home. I took a right turn into Putnam, went passed the first traffic light, and continued to the next at which I should take a left onto Whitney Avenue. There was a very tall truck ahead of me and I could not see the lights. Every time the truck moved I followed. The truck took a left on to Whitney Avenue and I followed. One more traffic light and I would be home. The very tall truck went through the lights and I followed. The light had changed to red but the truck went though and I kept going. That's when I heard a big thud on the right broad side of the car. A child waiting to cross had broken loose from the father's tight grip of his hand and run across Whitney Avenue. The child lay limp on the road motionless and mute. A hostile crowd gathered, and some were peering into my car. I don't own a cell phone and could not call for help. The police arrived. In the meantime, an ambulance had arrived and taken the lad away. The police officer asked me to produce the license which I had left at home. I said I live hundred yards away I could fetch it. They said that will not do.

"Sir, you ran the red light, you hit a child who has been taken to the Emergency Room and you do not have your license with you. We have to arrest you. Sorry."

Oh my god, I have ten kilos of marijuana in the trunk. What'll I do?

That's when I screamed, "Oh my god!"

That woke my wife.

14

Meet Mother and Child

I'm talking to you
Just a minute, please, can't you see I'm talking?
I said, don't interrupt
What are you doing out of bed?
Go back to bed, I said
You can't watch in the afternoon
What do you mean, there's nothing to do?
Read the book you borrowed from the library
Take a sweater
What do you mean you don't need one?
Take one any way
If you don't, you are not going
Wipe your feet; wipe your feet. Do I have to tell you every time?
Hurry up; hurry up
Stop it, stop it, I said. I'll count up to ten
Go stand in the corner
Face the wall. I don't want to see you making faces
Clean up your room. Now I said now
What did you say?
Can I go out?
Repeat that
Can I go out, please?

That's better

Just a bite of salad

You don't always get what you want. Get used to it

Don't argue with me. I am not going to argue

Stop it

You didn't say please

Come here, give me a hug

Get to your room and stay there for ten minutes

No. One minute more

Have you done your homework?

Bring it here

Bring it here, please

That's enough

Once more and you are going home

Stop shouting from there; if you want to ask something, come close

I have to ask your father

I don't know when he'll be home.

Fasten your seat belt. All of you

I am sorry, that's the rule. You heard me

I don't want to hear any fighting

I hope you all went to the bath room

Stop giggling. I heard you

If you don't listen to me, you are going home now

Put that down and go outside

15

Beth, Barney and I

I was seated in the ophthalmologist's office waiting to be called. Two ladies came in and sat next to me. Friends it turned out. They were in their mid–sixties, I would say. They were frank, loud and open in their conversation. They were speaking in Spanish which I was able to follow. I gathered from the conversation one was Beth and the other Barney.

Many years ago, before Beth's husband died, she was abused by her husband, she confided. Beth said she could not leave the house except accompanied by the husband. She had to remain indoors. The only time she defied the husband was to secretively go to church and get back in haste. Beth's husband heard about this. He went to the church, dragged her out by the hair, took her home, and beat her she said.

"He was squeezing my neck when one of my children showed up. Only then he stopped."

"Why had you to put up with it?" Barney asked.

"I was afraid. I had no income of my own. My husband married me when I was twenty- two in Nicaragua and brought me here. I could not speak English and had no friends. Only after his death am I free to lead my own life. I have two children who are employed. I live with them."

Hearing this, my thoughts went back to my own life. When I was in high school I fell in love with a school mate. Against my parents' objections I moved in with him. We married and had three children in quick succession.

My husband was a religious and hardworking man. He changed. He cursed and beat me and went out drinking. I wanted to go back to school, but he was against it.

"Married women should stay at home, cook, clean house, and mind the children," he would say.

I longed for an education. So, I went to night school. One day he came drunk to my school and abused me in front of the other students. He would destroy my homework and other assignments, and I would have to do them all over again. He would hide my clothes.

Finally I finished high school and longed to go to a university. I had no money and had a ghost's chance of getting some from him. I heard the school I was attending was looking for someone to mop the floors, dispose trash, wash dishes and scrub toilets. I got the job. The school supervisor told me another school close-by was looking for someone to do the job I was doing, and he recommended me. I took on that job too.

I scrimped and saved and got my bachelor's degree. I was not satisfied. I wanted to study law. I believed a lawyer cannot be bullied. My professor encouraged me. He helped me to enroll. It was only after I became an attorney that I was able to support myself and the kids. Until then I stomached all the humiliation and bore all the abuses, very often physical.

I felt it was time I left this man who I was convinced will never change. I divorced him.

I hear the medical assistant call my name. I must go.

16

The man who could not sleep

He twists and turns in his bed. Just cannot go to sleep. He tosses and turns. He twists the sheets. Still cannot sleep. He remembers about counting sheep. The sheep keep on coming. No end in sight. Puts on the light and reads. He watches television. He makes a warm drink with plenty of cream and sugar even though he is on a diet. It does not help. His wife is visiting her sister in Canada. He calls her and complains as though that would help. She suggests he go to the all-night gym and tire himself out. He still cannot sleep. He goes to see his doctor. The doctor examines him, talks a lot and prescribes, and suggests he have a physical and chest x-ray followed by a fat bill.

He cannot take it anymore.

He takes the loaded revolver and blows out his brains. He thinks he's dead but his eyes are still wide open.

17

If only

Charlie was young, free and ambitious with an imagination that had no limits. He was determined to change the world. He really believed he could.

As he grew older he became wiser. To his chagrin he discovered the world would not change the way he had imagined.

So, now wiser, Charlie lowered his sights and decided he would be satisfied if he merely changed the country. He worked hard at it. Even this seemed beyond his ability.

Charlie decided, "What the heck, I am the master of my house. I will change my family to my ways." Alas! They would have none of it. They had plans of their own.

Now Charlie on his deathbed reflects: "If only I had changed myself first, then perhaps by example I would have changed my family and they theirs with a better chance of changing the country and perhaps even the world.

18

Obstinate dad

He doesn't care. He must catch the flight. That's all that matters.

I cannot take this anymore. My nerves begin to get jumpy. I could hear my heart beat inside my ears. I take my cell phone from my purse and call the police and give them our location. "Please officer! If you don't get here soon there are going to be several deaths"

My husband does not hear me. His eyes are fixed on the road. I keep looking back for the police car. I see one approaching and then hear the siren.

"It's the police," I tell my husband.

What a relief when I hear the alarm clock go off.

19

Fear

I was burdened with fear. Fear was my constant companion. Feared the dark, feared choking, feared dying. There was no getting away from fear for me.

Every time I board a plane I am convinced there is a bomb in the hold. There is only one question in my mind – when will I be blown up? I have nothing to indicate there is a bomb, and yet I am terrified. With increasing paranoia I walk up and down the aisle, arousing the curiosity of flight attendants and fellow passengers. Many a time I have been told, "Sir, you should get back to your seat." I get into the bathroom and splash water on my face. I am constricted by fear. I sweat profusely, expecting the bomb in the hold might go off anytime."

The bomb does not go off.

As planned, I check in at the hospital. I have to share the room with a heart patient. His wife, Amazonian in construction, is visiting him. She comes in daily. "What are you here for?" he asks hesitantly.

"Suspected of brain tumor," I say. They whisper. "Is it terminal?" she asks shyly. "I have no idea. I should know soon"

"Brain tumor," the husband whispers. They nudge each other lovingly.

I know what they are thinking. They want my heart.

In the days that followed the husband and wife are nice to me. She brings me fruits.

After the surgery I fly home. I think of them quite often.

20

Waiting for his turn

There were three very old men who shared one room in the nursing home. They were seriously ill and confined to bed. This room had only one window. The window was the only link to the outside world. Charles was the most senior and his bed was next to the window. The other two were Tony and David, seniority in that order. Charles died and Tony being the next in seniority was moved to the bed next to the window. Tony, lying in bed, would describe to David all he could see through the window. The policeman on his beat, the pretty women on the sidewalk, the hawkers plying their wares, children traipsing to school, the intense activity at the fire station--on and on he would go. He would give names to the women and kids he saw. "Today Nancy is wearing a beautiful spotted dress. Little Lilly is crying, and the mother is pacifying her."

He would describe them with such gusto that David could not take it any longer. He wanted the bed badly. And he knew the only way he could occupy the bed by the window was if Tony died.

Tony had a bad heart; and when he had an attack in the night. he would reach for the pills on a tripod between their beds.

In the middle of the night David moved the pills out of Tony's reach. Tony had a severe attack and died. David was now moved to the bed by the window, the bed for which he had committed murder.

Eagerly, as soon as he was tucked in, he looked out. All he could see was the blank wall of a tall building.

21

By the way

Her husband had died a few years ago and she was lonely. She could no longer maintain the house, however modest it was. She moved into a condominium complex. Every evening around the same time she would take a walk, swinging both arms, along Whitney Avenue for exercise, fresh air, and just to be out in the open.

Before long she would often see this youthful gentleman coming in the opposite direction. He, by no means a virgin, had dated sporadically but that also half-heartedly. They would exchange smiles and proceed on their separate ways. As the days rolled by, they began to greet each other, saying, "Have a good day" and "Good night." As more days went by they would pause for a while and discuss the weather. Now they began walking in the same direction, and at the end of the road before they parted he would gently kiss her *"Good Night."*

It was pretty clear to them they enjoyed each other's company and looked forward to the walk down Whitney Avenue.

One day after summoning sufficient courage and with casual indifference he said to her, "We all have unfulfilled desires. What's yours?"

"My husband was a good man. He worked two jobs and provided for me to the best of his ability. We dreamed of owning an apartment on Fifth Avenue, going to all the plays and concerts, spending the weekend evenings walking in Central Park."

Many more weeks went by. One day he said, "If it means so much to you, why don't we both go by train to New York City, walk along Fifth Avenue, and see a play"

"I'd love to!" she said.

Standing in front of a row of apartments on Fifth Avenue, he asked, "Which catches your fancy?"

"That one there."

"It's yours."

He was a big- time real estate developer who owned vast amounts of property in New York City.

22

Thirty Fourth- Floor

Tim and Tom arrived in New York City from London on an assignment from their company. They were given ten days to complete the job.

They decided they would work night and day, complete the job in nine days, and use the tenth day to experience the City's night life.

They worked very hard and completed their assignment in nine days. They occupied the thirty fourth floor. On the ninth day, they informed the hall porter that they would be returning very late, very likely in the wee hours of the morning.

"Remember, gentlemen," the porter warned. "From twelve to five in the morning the elevator power is turned off. Come prepared to walk the thirty- four floors. You are on your own."

"Don't you worry, sir! We will be in excellent spirits, 'spiritually revived' we will not feel it."

They went bar hopping, visited as many night clubs as their funds would permit, and arrived at their apartment complex at two in the morning completely swished.

In order to make their trudge up less arduous they agreed, like the pilgrims in Chaucer's Canterbury Tales traveling from Southwark to Canterbury, to tell stories to pass the time. Tim and Tom agreed that each of them would relate a story, and as soon as one finished his story the other must come up with his. If not, a fifty-dollar penalty would be levied.

It was agreed.

The plan proceeded smoothly. On the entrance to their apartment on the thirty fourth floor Tim said to Tom, "We have an early morning flight to catch. Let's get in and catch some sleep."

"Oh My God!" cried out Tom. "The room key is in the car glove box."

23

Never be too good.

Don Michael and Charlie Kuns were extremely close friends. So, when Don Michael was dying, Charlie Kuns said to Don, "Could I accompany you up to the pearly gates."

"Sure! If it's not too much of a bother, I'd love it," replied Don Michael.

At the gates Charlie stood aside and watched.

The gatekeeper asked Don Michael his full name, last address, his social security number, date of birth, and the names of his relatives who had preceded him. The gatekeeper turned the pages of the manual in his possession and found all Don Michael's answers to be correct.

Finally, the gatekeeper asked, "What was your occupation?"

"Singer, sir" Don Michael replied.

"Singer? What kind of songs?" the gatekeeper inquired.

"Calypso"

"Never heard of it. Let me hear it," ordered the gatekeeper.

Don Michael sang "Day O," the Banana Boat Song, the "Jamaica Farewell," "Jump in the line," "I do adore her," "Brown Skin Girl," and on and on. He's still there at the gates singing.

Fed up Charlie Kuns returned to earth.

24

"What's going on?"

One day, Premadasa found himself walking along a road which he guessed was Galle Road, recognizing some of the familiar shops. He had no clue how he got there or where he came from or where he was heading. He did not know what time it was.

The road was completely deserted. Finally, he saw a lady approaching him.

"Lady, may I know the time, please?" he asked.

The lady gave him one look, screamed, and took to her heels.

Pedestrians coming in the opposite direction on sighting him ran to the other side of the road.

Strange! I must get home soon and find out what is happening, thought Premadasa

He hailed a taxi. The taxi driver gave him one look, banged the door shut, and took off.

"I must get someone from home to meet me here and take me home, please god," he wailed.

He telephoned his wife. A voice he could not recognize answered.

"May I speak to Agnes Premadasa, please."

"She is at a funeral right now. She cannot be reached."

"Whose funeral?" Premadasa inquired.

"Mr. Premadasa's" was the reply

"How did he die?"

"Mr. Premadasa died of bullet wounds."

"Any talk as to who may have done it."

"The name Wijewardene is bandied about, sir"

25

The Importance in being Tiny

"Heaven lies about us in our infancy."
William Wordsworth

I am in my library. A small room, call it a throw- away from the living quarters.

When I am here I'm left alone. The two monsters that scramble my serenity are banished from here: the clock that turns my head and neck every now and then and the telephone that jerks me out of my happy reverie.

This is the inner sanctum wherein I accost my other self, the small voice that carries a big stick. This is where I conduct a frank dialogue with him. This is where my hopes lie abandoned, my dreams deferred, my fears, my follies, my foibles, griefs, humiliations, the teeming recollections of past days, weeks, even years are laid bare. My thoughts often flash back to Howard Roark's brilliant defense in Ayn Rand's "Fountainhead."

"Hold it Hold it. You sound very erudite. Tell me all about it."

"The primary act – the process of reason – must be performed by each man alone. We can divide a meal among many men. We cannot digest it in a collective stomach. No man can use his lungs to breathe for

another man. No man can use his brain to think for another. All the functions of body and spirit are private. They cannot be shared or transferred."

In fact, my good friend, in here I reflect on everyone, anyone, anything and everything that the mind can get its arms around.

"Fortunately, you don't have a big mind. Anyway, you like this place, ah!"

Of course, I do. You know that. It's like a dream.

"A dream did you say. A dream is the mind playing tricks. What happens here is real."

The trouble with you is you are not responsive to the subtleties of distinction.

"Sometimes you talk above my head. Please explain."

All that I witness in a dream is personal to me. No one else can ever be privy to it unless I choose to reveal it. In a dream time is on freeze. Here I keep time hand-cuffed. Isn't this what takes place here?

"Now I get you."

Finally!

From where I am seated I can see lined up against the wall my favorite books. The complete works of you know who, a couple of Dickens, "Rag Time," "The Bridges of Madison County," "For Whom the Bell Tolls," Robert Penn Warren's "All the King's Men." Not many because I lean heavily on the munificence of the public library.

"You stingy bastard!"

I pay my taxes and am entitled to its rewards.

It's a sunny afternoon. I would say around two o'clock. The computer has been booted up. There is a file balanced on my lap.

"Why then this long face?"

You speaking to me?

"Who else? You are the only one here."

You don't have to rub it in. I heard you.

"Tell me I'm all ears. like Ross Perot."

I am thirty-one years old. I am head of my department. I have twelve people reporting to me and I report directly to the C.E.O. Some of those in my department are older than my dad.

"So what? If you don't like it, beat it, man."

I must get on the board before I am thirty-five, and I am going to do whatever it takes to get there.

"I've heard all this before. A few more questions. Does your staff like you?"

Kind of neutral I would say. They won't fall on a sword for me. Neither will they rat on me, I think.

"How about the C.E.O.? Does he like you?"

You're asking a lot of questions, aren't you?

"I am on a listening tour like Hillary and Bush before the elections."

I think the C.E.O. recognizes my loyalty, my meeting deadlines, my punctuality bordering on the punctilious. The usual tribal marks of an eager corporate executive, one who aspires to the top of the totem pole.

"You mean food chain."

Whatever!

"So why then this long-face?"

You dumb ass, you oaf. This is what happened. Murphy's Law took me by the collar and shook me all day.

"You look it. You look like Murphy's identical twin. Go on."

Yesterday I woke up in shock. It was seven A.M. My usual time by the alarm is five. I had an important meeting, chaired by the C.E.O, with the heads of the departments at nine. On a good day it takes me forty- five minutes to drive to the office. I had an hour and a quarter to get the wheels rolling along Merritt Parkway. After a flash shit, shave, and shampoo, I grabbed a tie and jacket and was at the car at ten past eight. Not bad, eh? Christ!

"Don't swear!"

Shut up and listen. The left front tire was flat. I installed the donut, soiling the cuffs of my starched white shirt, and entered the Merritt at twenty-five past eight. Christ!

"Here you go again, swearing and taking the Lord's name in vain."

For Christ's sake shut up.

"What now? Go on."

The cars were nose-to-butt, nose-to-butt like dogs in heat in the summer.

"Man, could you not have used a more kosher analogy, ah?"

Kosher or Halal, you got the picture, didn't you? You know something. I am going to ignore you or order you out. Buzz off.

"Fat chance, my friend. I will always be with you. I reside in your skin. I'll pinch and poke you like you do to fruits in the super market. I'll not slavishly follow you like Ruth. 'Your people shall be my people, your God my God,' blah, blah. On the contrary I shall challenge you to do better. I'll chastise you when you err, as I did when at your staff meeting you were condescending and humiliated Joe. I shall congratulate you and make you feel good whenever you do the right thing. As for instance when you fought tooth and nail like a Gurkha for Emma's promotion and substantial pay rise."

You mean like Mister Jeeves and Bertie Wooster; Doctor Watson and Sherlock Holmes?

"I think I do a better job. They are ephemeral. I have gravitas. They are fiction. I am real. I'm your D.N.A. Through me you can be tracked and identified. You digress. Get to the point."

Then stop interrupting me.

As I was saying I was on the Merritt and I checked the radio. Some fat (I think) hombre has had cardiac arrest, and so there are rubber necks in and out of every car window just like, you know, the annoying cuckoo in the cuckoo clock.

"It looks like cuckoo for you. Go on."

The building elevator is out of order and so I begin to run up the stairs, one, two, three and by the time I reached the ninth floor I was dripping with sweat. I enter my office at quarter past nine. My assistant comes running to me. "The meeting has started and the C.E.O. has been on the phone twice," he says. I grab the file and enter the board room. I spot the only chair unoccupied at the far end. Like the cat that drinks milk, I close my eyes in the belief that "if I can't see, others can't see me." I inch sideways sashaying between chairs and wall and take

my seat. Oh Krishna. What have I done? I hope you are happy now.
No more Christ.

"Christ or Krishna what now"

I see you are really curious. You won't believe what I had done.

"Spit it out man. Spit out. You're killing me."

I've brought the wrong file. I shuffle out of the board room. Like a
back itch I cannot reach I feel the scorn of everyone.

"So? Why the long face? These things happen to a lot of people. A
comma may be in a person's career, not a period. Go on"

Wish it were so simple, brother. My proposal was blasted to bits.

"By whom may I ask?

By that roadside bum Tony, who wakes up every morning scheming
how to do me in come what may.

"That's really sad. Up to this point you were the victim of accidental
circumstances. Quite understandable I would say. A bad presentation,
Aha! No way Jose! You have a lot of mopping up to do my friend. How
did you feel when the meeting adjourned?"

You really want to know?

"You heard me."

I felt like that Menorah under a giant tree: "Hello! Hello! I'm here."
But nobody seems to care.

Fifty weeks of toil and tedium. Fifty weeks of routine taking the
same route, seeing the same familiar cars ahead of me with the same
bumper stickers: "We do not have a democracy we have an auction."
"Whisky is risky." "My ex -wife in the trunk." Fifty weeks of trying to
get ahead while protecting my back. Fifty weeks of deadlines, dead-ends
and dealing with dead-enders. And all for what, pray? Two weeks of
vacation. And how do you think we spend the vacation?

"You tell me. You are the one who goes on vacations."

Drive to Kennedy, threading through traffic, arriving four hours
before departure. Shuffle-shuffle with bursting bags to reception and
heave the bags on the scale. The damsel at reception, eyes me with bored
indifference. And then reminded of her in-house training fiat to be nice
to patrons, she flashes a fatuous smile. And with the same enthusiasm

as a flight attendant explaining the use of oxygen masks, she blabbers, "Did you leave your bags unattended any time – did you pack your bags – have a pleasant flight." Reminds me of the Super Stop and Shop girl's "havagooday."

I walk up to security check. Do you know what goes through my mind?

"What?"

Oscar Wilde.

"Oscar Wilde? You mean Uranian love, the love that dares not speak its name."

Is that all you know of Oscar Wilde? You should be ashamed of yourself.

"Then what pray?"

When at customs Oscar Wilde was asked whether he had anything to declare, he replied with that signature smirk of his, "I have nothing to declare except my genius." I think of this every time I approach the security check.

"That my friend is the closest you will ever get to being a genius."

Thanks. What a buddy you are.

I bare everything except my soul at the security check.

"You've got a soul? I thought long ago you had sold it to mammon."

Shut up.

I sit pretzel like in the aircraft for over six hours. Take two steps at a time to baggage claim which has a mind of its own. Elbow fellow travelers to get vantage point to stare at the capricious carousel which will come up with my bags slower than Shylock a shekel and, before I can say, "Jack Daniel" I'm doing it all over again returning home after living out of suit cases, fat, flatulent, and over stuffed, promising to spend more time at the gym.

"I must say this much for you. You're having a heck of a time."

If you have any suggestions let me have them. If not, shove your comments.

While driving home, thoughts of office take hold of me. Has anyone placed an Improvised Explosive Device in my office during my absence?

I think about the extra hours I will have to put in to catch up with the load of work that was piling up. The office motto must have been "put it on his desk!"

And now I have to redo this project presentation and have it signed, sealed and sent by Monday. Just not up to it, my friend. Just not up to it at all. I feel like what the cat refused to bring in.

"How would you know what the cat refused to bring would look like if the cat did not bring it in?"

Shut up.

Do you remember Alberto Moravia's "A Bad Winter"?

"Of course, I do. We read it together."

You remember the protagonist not wishing to marry Clara to whom he was engaged saying, "How on earth can I manage to spend my whole life at close quarters with a woman who is so inert, so frozen, so unfeeling?"

"Alberto Moravia must have had Rosie O'Donnell in mind, although Rosie is anything but a frozen chick. Anyway, I do not see the relevance. Go on."

Subtleties! Subtleties! And you say you read the story. Here's the relevance, you nit wit. He wails, you remember, "The violence of my repentance made me want to beat my head against the wall. I'm finished: I've buried myself alive. I'm dead and under the ground. My life is over." Never again shall I hope to get on the board. This is how I feel right now, my friend.

"I'm waiting to see how you come out of this one."

I hear the door open. Face, dress and fingers all covered with chocolate, she enters with faltering steps like sudden sunshine on a cloudy day; defying all gloomy weather predictions, she rushes the three yards and leaps into my lap. In seconds she is gurgling with that innocence to which I supplicate in silence. Totally! Absolutely!

Tiny is now in full control. No laws can apply to her and she knows it. Like the Queen of England, she can do no wrong when she is with her daddy and she is aware of it. She taps the keyboard with her chocolate fingers. She dials imaginatively and purrs "hello, hello," she scribbles on all the blank papers she can get hold of and, leaving me all "chocolatty," she wafts away just as abruptly as she appeared. She is off to her next prank, secure in the embrace of parental love.

"You felt good, didn't you?"

I felt like the boxer who has got a severe walloping, wobbly on his feet, bruised and bloody, hearing the bell signaling the end of the round.

"In boxing parlance they call it "saved by the bell.""

There you go again showing off.

As I watch her I realize although this tiny four- year old is in full control of our lives from the time she cries out of bed in the morning to the time she is carried back to bed at night, she is in fact totally dependent on me for what she is to become. I could by assiduous labor turn her into a diva doing good, like say Oprah; by selfish neglect a treacherous Delilah or just permit her to drift into becoming just one more mediocrity among the faceless millions everywhere.

Such is the awesome power I have over her life. A power checked only by the painful awareness of the grave consequences of my actions.

I felt a sudden burst of physical energy, the competitive spirit in me like a sacred mantra passed on by my fore-fathers, from sire to son by word of mouth, spanning generations back and beyond, like mother's milk that runs through the veins of every child is awakened and takes hold of me. I'm all fired up.

"Hold it! Hold it! What's gotten into you? You aren't the same person I saw walk in here."

In dire situations like this, my good friend, it has happened before. I'm transformed into a gladiator.

"Why not say bull fighter, a matador--that is more current. Few people have heard of a gladiator."

This is my story. Ok?

My mind becomes a clenched fist like the black power salute. My spine turns to steel. My resolve more Churchillian than Martin Luther K or Mahatma Gandhi.

I pick up the file tossed away by Tiny and dig in. Like the ant which when its nest collapses, immediately with alacrity sets about building another and better I get to work with a passion that takes full possession of me. I vow that my next presentation will wow them all.

And it did.

Now I am on the fast track to a seat on the board. Aren't you going to ask me how I feel?

"Tell me about it."

Immense happiness weighed me down. Happiness stirred in my breast, spontaneously. First it was small and rolled about like a rubber ball on a polished wooden floor making it difficult to locate it. You know it's there, somewhere but not exactly where. Then there was no mistaking. It swelled broader and bigger and surged like a wave. The good feeling moved from breast to arms and legs and I felt it right here in my bones. Everything about me trembled, trembled with pure joy. "Lord how marvelous."

Thanks, Tiny. You made me do it.

"Don't get carried away young man. Your nemesis Tony is quite alive and well."

Vincent Van Goh about his little nephew:

"What amazes me most is that such a little child has so much personality, against which you are utterly powerless. Now and then he looks at me as if he wanted to say, "What are you doing to me – I know much more about things than you do." His are the eyes of an adult and then with a lot of expression."

26

Single and Solitary

"O solitude! Where are the charms
That sages have seen in thy face?"
William Cowper

B eing single is harder on the woman than the man, especially on those who do not have the ballast of families dear to them, living close to them. Those who were never married or committed and have remained single throughout do not feel the void caused by the absence of the spouse. They carry on as always. There are over twenty-five million singles we are told – widowed, divorced or never committed.

Men who seldom outlive women appear to cope much better. Very often they are able to shop around and find a female companion in similar circumstances. A man alone looks carefree, bold and dashing while a woman alone looks more like a lamb left behind, bleating for help.

Single women must constantly keep checking for signs of disintegration, depression, and dementia. It is paramount not to be overcome by sorrow, to continue to stay sane. It seems at first the condition is temporary, that this too will pass. Feelings of insecurity and isolation, days segueing into nights without human contact. Then it will dawn on her, creep upon her, that very likely it's going to be permanent for the rest of her life.

For a single woman sadly, America is not the place to be, America is short of friendly public places. The French have their cafes, the British the pubs, the sunny Latin countries the open air, but here in America the singles have to settle for malls which have been taken over by rambunctious teenagers.

It's inconvenient, this solitary life. Silence ticks like a bomb. Solitaires talk at length to themselves, to their pets, even to the television and telephone. The ring of the telephone is not a nuisance; it's a welcome, to be grabbed eagerly for, establishing human contact. A solitary woman feels like the tree falling in the silence of the forest, alone in a room, nobody around, a loneliness you feel when love is withheld from you like the restlessness of hunger in the smell of food. It's terrifying.

Inspiration in solitude may be a major commodity for poets and philosophers: "tongues in trees, books in running brooks, sermons in stones, and good in everything. I would not change it." But not for those who are single and solitary. In short, there's constant anxiety.

"Like one that on a lonesome road doth walk in fear and dread,
        And having once turned around, walks on,
              And turns no more his head;
          Because he knows a frightful fiend
            Doth close behind him tread"
                  – Coleridge

The single woman would pick up the newspaper at the entrance, let herself into her apartment with half a loaf of bread and a can of corned beef; and calling for the pet, she would stare down the unblinking light on the answering machine and then perhaps make a cup of tea and settle down to read through the junk mail. Work for her is not a tiresome chore. She immerses herself in work brought home from office; and if there be none, she would rearrange the kitchen cabinet or the clothes closet.

A single person feels it most painfully in circumstances such as these. Nobody lends a hand. She cannot say: "Would you get the door for me -- hand me the towel – hold up the other end? – go see what's making that funny noise – answer the phone -- mail a letter – pick-up the prescription -- withdraw money from the bank." Hanging a picture becomes a frustrating undertaking. She punches a dozen more holes in the wall than necessary because no one will stand across the room to guide her. No one to give a hand to carry in the groceries or carry out the trash. If the couch is too heavy to move, it must wait where it is until a strong person should come over on a totally unconnected errand.

At the dining table she turns around to share a joke or an important happening only to find there's nobody there, nobody to share the small change of complaints and observations we enjoy indulging in {like to say how narrowly she missed having an accident, that it's getting darker earlier or the latest Trump faux pas.} No one to remind her she is wearing one sock black and the other blue, no one to remind her to turn the clock back and forward. To be invited to a birthday party and not be able to return the pleasure.

To be alone but not lonely, alone on purpose, having rejected company by choice rather than having been cast out--we are told that's the American badge of a hero, the lone explorer – "Dr. Livingstone I presume" – the cowboy who saves a village and rides away into the sun set – the prototype American hero like Alan Ladd in Shane ("Shane, come back! Shane!") or Gary Cooper in "High Noon," romanticized without any connection to reality. It is easy to pontificate as Sir Philp Sidney did, "They are never alone that are accompanied by noble thoughts." Tell that to a single woman.

Only a solitary woman knows the joys of friendship. To one who is single and solitary her friends are everything. If necessity is the mother of invention, here you have it. In Toronto, Canada, drawing sustenance from Mathew 10: 29 ("Are not two sparrows sold for a farthing? One of them shall not fall on the ground without your Father" KJV) a friendly, sororal band of single women formed the well-known "Sparrows" who are always ready, eager, and committed to come to each other's assistance.

Loneliness if left untreated, is not only psychically painful, it is now firmly believed it can have debilitating medical consequences like heart disease, cancer and depression leading to suicide. No wonder, to the relief of many in the United Kingdom, Prime Minister Theresa May appointed a "minister for loneliness" who will be tackling what she calls "the sad reality of modern life"

Facebook and Instagram with all their claims of thousands of friends and followers has resulted in social disconnection as they lack the warmth and nearness of old fashioned one-on-one human contact. Loneliness and isolation are hardest on the poor, the unemployed, and the displaced migrant population as their lives are unstable and so are their relationships.

Author Joyce Maynard in "Strangers in the House" allows a peek into her situation. She comes home from the airport sometime after the death of her husband, and "by the time I reached the house, I was so weary I set down my suitcase and went straight to bed." That night she was robbed, credit cards and all. "After the last of the police officers had driven off . . . I was still working on how a person moves on when the partner she loved won't be there anymore. That morning I felt like calling to the sky, "For God's sake, Jimmy! Where are you? And why aren't you here?"

And more:

By Kathleen Volk Miller in "A Future Without Him."

We heard the strangest sounds coming from the front porch, a squawking and an unworldly scream. The children fled into the kitchen, scared and yelling, which is what I wanted to do, too. But I had to handle whatever this was.

I looked out to see our family cat, Echo, with a cardinal in her mouth that was flapping and screeching, struggling to get out. My first thought was to call my husband, followed by a realization: I couldn't. A month earlier, he had died. I still wake up every morning feeling stunned by this new reality.

27

Supermarket

I'm standing in the express check-out lane at the nearby grocery store I patronize once a week, balancing a dozen eggs on top of a twelve-pack carton of cokes, when the lady in front of me dumps her purse out on the counter.

"I've a coupon for these cookies," she tells the clerk.

Forcing a smile, the clerk looks at me and then beyond me at the other people doing their own balancing acts.

"I've got it," the patron shouts.

"This is for ShopRite cookies." says the clerk. "You have the original ones."

"But I have a coupon for this. I put it in my purse this morning. Give me a few minutes."

Meanwhile, my arm is starting to get numb so I shove my stuff behind her groceries on the automatic belt, which is now painfully motionless. The clerk tosses me one of those plastic dividers. The people behind me start to groan; some of them go off to the regular lane where people are purchasing fifty items or more.

The insouciant customer merrily sorts through a fist full of crumpled coupons, lip gloss, face powder, wallet, checkbook, assortment of gum and candy bars, cell phone, receipts, and more.

I heard someone whisper, "She forgot the kitchen sink." What I saw was a museum of knickknacks.

"Here, lady," I say as I hand her a five- dollar bill. "Let me pay the difference. No. let me pay for the whole pack of cookies. It's my treat. Just please can we get this line moving."

"I beg your pardon. You don't have to be rude and insulting," she says to me. Loudly!

"Never mind," she tells the clerk. "I won't get them."

After the clerk bags the rest of her groceries and the lady leaves the store taking two steps at a time, I look down at the floor and notice the coupon for ShopRite cookies she had been looking for.

Should I run out to the parking lot and try to find her?

Forget it.

28

Baby sitter

"You do not have to change the diaper," they told Marissa emphatically. "You can be quite sure Timothy will not wake while we are at the movies."

"He is a very sound sleeper," they assured her.

No need to have a bottle for him or anything. In fact, she was not expected to do anything at all. Before the Clintons left they said firmly, "Please do not look in on the sleeping baby. He'll be all right."

"That's funny" she said to herself.

After two hours of reading all of the boring mail piled on the table (none addressed to her, of course), watching television (which her parents would have forbidden) looking through a wedding album filled with photographs of dressed-up people, and finishing most of the M&Ms on the table, she was bored.

She now became curious.

She stood outside the door and tried to hear the sound of the baby breathing, but she couldn't hear anything through the door except the sound of the occasional car that passed by on the street outside. She wondered what Timothy looked like. She wasn't even sure how old he was. Why had she agreed to baby-sit when Mr. Clinton approached her at the swimming club? Why—because the two families were friends.

She tiptoed and very quietly opened the door. What did she see?

The room was empty. They had left the bed just as their child had made it. The small blue desk was littered with colored pencils and scraps of art paper, a bottle of white glue, and assorted toys.

There was a picture of a pretty baby held closely to Mrs. Clinton's chest.

She heard the sound of an approaching car. She ran and sat in the living room.

Mrs. Clinton went directly to the baby's room. She heard the door close. She heard the sound of sobbing emanating from the room.

Mr. Clinton drove Marissa to her home without a word between them. "She'll be O.K.," he said while Marissa was getting out of the car.

29

Pickpocket

Tired of losing his wallet to pickpockets, Anton, now eighty, decides to teach at least one pickpocket a lesson he will remember for a long time. He takes an old wallet, stuffs it with expired lottery tickets, chewing gum wrappers, and old receipts from the trash bin. The wallet is now fat and inviting. "All hat and no cattle. This oyster has no pearl. Who steals my purse steals trash" he mumbles with a canted smile.

He sets out to practice.

Standing in front of a full- length mirror he practices his act. With a walking stick for support he walks unsteady with a stoop, occasionally tapping his hip pocket to draw attention.

With his friend Soros, they go to the same mall and store where once before his pocket had been picked. Soros was to wait for him. It's like a getaway car. As soon as his pocket is picked, he will get to the car and they will head for home.

Anton ponderously approached a bargain counter where many shoppers were milling around; and while examining a tie closely, he feels he is being relieved of his wallet. With a smile, he prepares to take off.

Just then he hears a shop assistant screaming "Sir, Sir, don't go. This man here has stolen your wallet. Here he is," and she points to the man holding the wallet in his hand. Anton, anxious to scram out of there, stammers, "As long as I have the wallet back, I will be happy."

At this point a crowd had gathered and they all agree the matter should be handed over to the police. There have been too many such thefts, the shoppers contend. Because of all the commotion the mall security turns up, and he escorts the two of them and the witnesses to his office.

Soros tired of waiting takes off.

"The best laid plans of mice and men often go awry."

30

Airport

Once at Bradley airport while I was waiting to meet a friend who did not turn up, a woman accosted me, saying in a familiar tone, "It's been a long time. How have you been?" The enthusiasm of her embrace seemed misplaced.

I had no idea who she was but refrained from revealing my ignorance of her identity.

She offered to drive me to my hotel. I told her I had to make a very brief surprise call on my fiancé; and as we approached the house, we could see my fiancé in the garden in the amorous embrace of a man.

"Do you still want to see her?" she asked.

"No, let's get out of here," I said.

She suggested dinner, to which I gladly agreed.

She said she was in sales and was returning from a trip to Canada. She appeared to have done well. At dinner, she ordered glass after glass of wine and yet remained sober. She recalled things that happened to me that had never occurred and people we both knew well whom I hadn't known at all. As she spoke, her thoughts seemed to arrive. "You've lost weight," she said, and I had no idea what she was talking about. It finally dawned on me she had mistaken me for someone else.

Back in the car, she turned off the air conditioning, took out a plastic bag filled with white powder, and held it out. "Pharmaceutical grade, you know what to do. You have done it before. Here's a thousand. Beat it before the cops spot us."

So saying, she put me out of the car and drove off in her Corvette.

I saw a man in the parking lot and recalled the name of a boy in high school who looked like me. We were often confused with each other. The man in the parking lot passed me. I saw him get into a car and drive off.

31

The Handbag

There is a thief whose specialty is snatching handbags from elderly women shopping on Fifth Avenue in New York City. He had made a name for himself as a professional.

Today he is targeting Anne Coulter. She is eighty-two years old. He intends to snatch her handbag by applying the usual quick, powerful jerking motion.

Now, what frequently happens in these situations is, that the elderly ladies, out of sheer fright, forget to release their grip on the hand bag and are pulled to the ground, whereupon they invariably acquire an injury before they finally let go of the strap and the robber then runs away.

Completely different, however, is the case with stubborn eighty-two year-old Anne Coulter.

It doesn't even occur to her to let go of the handbag. As a consequence, the snatcher is compelled to drag the old lady behind him through the crush of shoppers, diagonally across the extensive lawns of Central Park—yes, through the entire inner city, straight onto a commuter bus and right out again. This continues for hours on end until the Snatcher, who is really a strong and athletic young man, can barely continue due to exhaustion, and so he finally has to come to a standstill in the middle of a street in Brooklyn Heights.

This, of course, is the moment that eighty-two year-old Coulter has been waiting for and for which the thief did not bargain. In a jiffy she bounces back to her feet, and now it's her turn to drag the horrified snatcher behind her until she is so tired she can't continue anymore, and then it's his turn again.

The morning, noon and evening news on all the channels covered this saga. Children came running home from school to watch it on television. Families after supper settled down to watch it. Bets were being taken at bars as to who will throw in the towel.

It has been going on for eighteen months now and people are beginning to suspect that there's something soft and sweet cooking between the two of them. It could also be a gimmick to advertise an Ivanka hand bag.

32

Moment OF Truth

Ron Carboom felt it was about time Rocky Sticks should know the facts. He knew it was going to be painful. And yet it had to be done. Ron was that kind of a man. Tell it as it is. Tell it but be gentle.

"Come on, Rocky," Ron said. "We need to talk. Let's go for a walk."

And off they went up the street, just the two of them, with Rocky falling behind now and then and needing to hurry to catch up. They wandered for a while in Edgerton Park in silence. Not a word between them. This is strange, very strange, Rocky thought. He's never like this. What's troubling him, Rocky wondered.

Ron sat on the bench and was quiet. He then held Rocky between his palms lovingly. "Look, Rocky, I've got to tell you. You are not our child. We love you as our own and always will. Remember that, always. You were picked out of a dumpster as a newborn."

Ron spared him the details. It was painful for both.

Then they went back home.

Rocky stopped at the foot of his favorite trees to leave behind his calling card, greeted the neighbors by wagging his tail, and barked at strangers. Today there was no bite in his bark.

33

Out sourced Fu

In the remote Ching-Chong village in the Fujian province Fu's mother and father go to work in the fields. From sun-up to moon rise Fu works from home like corporate executives in the United States.

He measures, cuts, shapes, punctures, and sews soccer balls. These balls then go rolling out of Ching-Chong village to the various soccer stadiums of the world.

Before he hands over the ball for inspection and payment he sticks a label on each of the balls.

"This ball was not made by children." He can neither read nor write. He has never been to school. Fu is twelve years old.

34

The Baby

A young couple was driving across a strip of desert. Strapped into a car seat between the couple was their nine month-old baby. After seven hours behind the wheel, the husband was beginning to get bleary-eyed.

"You look exhausted" the wife said. "Why don't you let me drive for awhile?"

"Thanks," the husband answered. "I could use a nap."

After an hour or so, the wife noticed the baby was missing.

"Oh my God!" the wife screamed. "Where's our child?"

Right across, they saw a police station. They both ran in and with the policeman came out to inspect.

The policeman laughed out loud.

This is what happened when trading driving places.

The husband slowed down and parked the car on the shoulder of the highway. The wife climbed out, lifted the baby out of the car saying, "Here move over."

"I can't," the husband said. "You've got to move that duffel bag you call purse out of the way first."

The wife then reached up and put the baby securely on the roof, threw the hand bag on the rear seat, checked herself in the mirror, said "Sleep as long as you want. I've everything under control," put the gear in drive, and took off.

35

I was a "Lift Boy!"

I am now 85 years old and I have long ago stopped buying green bananas. What I am recounting happened so long ago I cannot vouch for its veracity. It may even be woven out of whole cloth. There are times I walk into my bedroom and stand there staring at the bed or the wall trying to remember, "What did I come here for? What did I want to find? Perhaps in the other room." And yet there are lucid moments when the past unfolds vividly. I would like to believe this is one such moment. I wish I knew in advance how the incredible tale I have to tell will be received, whether as the raving of a crude imagination or as a recounting of the positive experience of a roving free spirit.

As the seventy year-old Mark Twain said to his biographer, Albert Bigelow Paine, "When I was younger I could remember anything, whether it happened or not; but I am getting old, and soon I shall remember only the latter."

My parents who were living in Federated Malay States at this time, sent me to Ceylon (that little island in the Indian Ocean cheek by jowl to South India).

One night after dinner my father called me over. My mother was seated next to him, and he was in a reclining chair. It was apparent to me that they had put their heads together in some serious back and forth.

My father's voice quivered and my mother was sobbing.

"Son," my father said tremulously, "You have missed a lot of schooling because of instability caused by rumors of an impending World War. Now it is certain the Japanese will invade this country and very likely take it over. You will be eighteen years old tomorrow. You must return to your roots. You need to get a sound education. The last boat leaves next week. You will be met by your uncle in Colombo and he will admit you to the best high school in your home town, Jaffna. You will live in the school hostel and on vacations visit your grandparents living in the neighboring village."

I did not hear a whisper from my mother. I think she passed out.

At high school I could not cope. I was too old for my class. And I dreaded tests. I manufactured excuses not to turn up for examinations. I decided to leave both school and home. I knew where my old and feeble grandparents kept their hard-earned savings—in an aluminum bowl. There were one thousand rupees. I took five hundred rupees and left a note written in Tamil – "This is a loan. I promise I'll pay it back."

With five hundred rupees in my pocket and just a change of clothes I set out for Colombo, the capital, in search of a job. I went directly to the Public library and scanned the wanted column in the dailies. "Wanted A Lift Boy," one said. I did not know what it meant. I turned up at the address. There was a queue waiting to be interviewed. I asked one of them what a lift was. It is a "car" (elevator to the reader) to take people up and down a tall building, he explained.

The interviewer, a gentleman in white short sleeves shirt, white pants and tie asked me, "What makes you think you'll like this job?"

"I am certain, sir. It'll be *very uplifting*" I replied.

He laughed. "When can you start working?" he asked.

"How about like now, sir," I answered.

The lift served, I think, six floors. I showed up at 8.30 in the morning and worked till 5.30 in the evening.

I wore a khaki uniform and sandals. No shoes. There was an hour break for lunch. I bought food from the push-carts one can find on the streets of the town of Pettah.

I noticed the lift was patronized entirely by white folk while the Ceylonese used the rear staircase. This continued for a while until one day a young Ceylonese lad entered the lift along with the white folks. The white men pretended not to notice him. I did not utter a word. I was warned I should keep my mouth shut and speak only when spoken to— and then only politely. The following day and the days thereafter more Ceylonese stepped into the lift. Remembering my boss's admonition to "speak only when you are spoken to," I kept my mouth shut but my eyes wide open. The lift was always packed to capacity – capacity meant when there was no more room to push-pack people in. Some would come smoking cigarettes and squish them with the heels of their shoes just outside the lift. Young men would walk to the back of the lift and pat or paw the protruding posteriors of female passengers. Some women would move away while others would stay on pretending nothing was happening. The white folk began using the staircase.

One day a white gentleman, who worked on the third floor for a stevedoring company and who always addressed me with "Good morning, young man," said I should see him in his office. During my lunch break I went over to see him. The secretary led me to his room and left me there. He was seated behind a large desk, and there were two telephones. Why two? I did not know then that one was an intercom.

"Look here, young man, there is a cargo boat leaving for Liverpool three days from today. They urgently need a Cabin Boy. If you are willing to scrub floors and handle slush buckets, the position is yours. What is more, you can travel free of charge. You will be discharged in Liverpool and thereafter you are on your own. If you are interested, see my secretary."

I was now gripped by the allure of being free. My mind had been in a constant, turbulent riot, burning to flee. I did not give a horse's patoot how my parents were going to miss me. Like Jay Gatsby I longed to "suck on the pap of life, gulp down the incomparable milk of wonder," break loose from the suffocating youthful boundaries, and set out for the land where Dick Whittington believed the streets were paved with gold.

I was on a cargo boat steaming towards Liverpool. Yes, I scrubbed the deck, polished brass and silver, and cleaned up the mess hall after the crew had had their meals. Though I did not love obedience, I never once questioned it. With head bowed, I performed all their commands. I was always busy, and I worked very hard to live. I had no hope of ever being rich enough to live a month without hard work, but God knows I was quite content. I had no prospect and I sought none.

Most of the time they called me "Boy," but there were those who called me by name. By and by they came to, I believe, like me. And yet . . . and yet there's one incident that stands out like a thumb, separate from others. Believe me when I say I bear no malice. What good would it do anyway? I was scrubbing the deck when one of the crew in a group playing cards, with others looking on, called out to me, "Boy!" I looked up and walked up to him. He raised his left leg. I did not understand. He stared at me and pointed at the leg again. Ah! I got it. The shoe lace had unraveled. I went down on my knees and knotted it. As I was getting back to my deck scrubbing, I heard them laugh.

At Liverpool I was spat out like one would spit out a seed after the flesh of the fruit had been eaten. And like a seed that will geminate on fertile soil, thereafter I took root in a different soil, which was Liverpool in England.

The crew, as I have said, took a liking to me towards the tail end of my passage. They sent the hat round among the workers and passengers and collected for me a princely sum of five hundred pounds sterling.

I did a myriad of jobs. Courier, night watchman at a public library, waiter at restaurants in the seedy parts of Soho, a bouncer at a strip club, and many more. So long as I didn't feel cold and I didn't feel hungry and I didn't feel thirsty, that was enough for me. My guiding philosophy was that if I cannot do good, at least "Do no harm."

I was longing to visit the Federated Malay States, the country of my birth. The Federated Malay States, having attained independence from the British, was now called Malaysia and so too Ceylon, the land of my progenitors, had changed its name to Sri Lanka. I was yearning to know whatever happened to my dear parents. They must have passed away, no doubt.

I had, exercising painful austerity, put away some money and after buying a cheap ticket set out for the Federated Malay States, now

Malaysia. Dear God! Nothing was familiar to me. Sentul, the little village where I was born, retained its name, but all else had changed. Tall buildings replaced the modest ones I was familiar with. The Railway Institute Club where I used to play table tennis while my father was hitting tennis balls was nowhere in sight. I stood there and cried, for the smells of your childhood will always stay with you and will make you remember home, whether you are scrubbing decks or washing dishes.

I wished I had spent my childhood doing something useful – something lasting. They say as you grow your dreams change as do your ideas about who you can be and what you want to accomplish during the short time you are alive. This did not happen to me. Humans are never satisfied. Give them one thing and they want something more. And yet, is this not what makes us humans different from animals. Animals are satisfied with what they have.

Standing there, I understood that each moment was a partition, with the past on one side and the future on the other, the future containing this unthinkable now. My life has been defined by suffering. I thought little of the future. It was all about the past—I pondered my mediocrity, the massive insignificance of my life, always asking myself what to keep of my past, what to bring to the future. Future? I am eighty-five years old. The past, as much as I can remember, went past me in slow motion. Actually, years whirred by in minutes. I began pitying myself – reviewing my past, reading it, interpreting it all. I have crossed too many worlds and lived too many lives. Memory fills my body as much as blood and bones. I have forgotten how to smile just as I have no further need for tears.

Every man in the world functions to the best of his ability, and no one does less than his best, no matter what he may think about it. As for me I have always sought succor in Shakespeare.

"There's a divinity that shapes our ends/ Rough hew them how we will."

A sense of loneliness crept over me. I felt the creeping of fate, the circling of the vultures of Karma. I had gone through pain and come out on the other side. I felt powerless. Life for me had been a series of unknowns, strung together, one after another, like the Hindu prayer beads (maalai) on a thread. I had embraced chance and danced with peril cheek-to-cheek. A life-long feeling of impoverishment and insecurity got hold of me.

How did I survive? Is it by the cunning instinct of the hunted or by just growing like a weed in an untended garden? I paced about my room, in the tiny motel in Sentul, my birth place, recalling, seldom smiling. Then my memories would merge into memories, nay reveries, and the past would mingle with the uncertainty of what's to come. In the end what is left, may I ask, of a life clipped and wingless, an absurdness from which there is no escape as though I was in a mad house of my own free will.

I missed my father and mother. However old one may be when one thinks of his parents, he becomes a child once more. I saw my mother's face again. I saw my father's face. There were only three of us by the last count. I was aware that this is only a moment. The world is waiting outside, as hungry as a tiger ready to devour me.

I decided to take a walk just to see the stars and the moon and to listen to the night. How true, it's only in the darkness of the night that one can see the stars and the moon.

I have known what it is to be hungry, cold, friendless, sick, and without a shilling in the world. I was yearning for a permanent place to settle down. I had no urge to return to Sri Lanka. There had been communal riots and many Tamils were leaving in a mad rush, mainly for Canada.

My itchy feet for travel began acting up. I realized I have become the "Wandering Jew."

I visited the Canadian embassy in Kuala Lumpur and applied for refugee status, which was swiftly granted.

I am now living in Scarborough in Toronto among my people in peace. And yet I live alone and I have no relatives. No wife or child. Never married. The family tree had no roots. Not anymore. I never lost my innocence. Big deal.

I have ended up just as I began. A thousand dollars in the bank and a nagging conscience, reminding me of an unsettled loan I had taken from my grandmother. I have heard about it. I have seen it from a polite distance, but I have not experienced what is called "ostentatious living." "Have the courage to appear poor," said Washington Irving, "and you disarm poverty of its sharpest sting."

Time reconciles us to anything. I gradually became content, doggedly content just like wild animals in cages.

No Horatio Alger, Ralph Lauren or George Soros for me.

But in my travels from ship to shore, surely there must have been something that gave me joy. When a cowboy gets into town, his first stop would be the bar. In my case it was the library. I could tell whether a town was safe or not from the condition of its library. I felt comfortable in a commodious, well stocked library. Like a mosquito's joy in a nudist colony, I would go from shelf to shelf, grab books and devour them. Herein I found unfettered joy.

36

The Three Sons

Dr. Robert Livingston and Mary had three sons. Their names were Patrick, Jonathan, and Neil. The parents saw to it they all graduated from reputable universities and were now on their own. This is how their lives unfolded.

Patrick marries his high school sweet heart Daphne. They are both immersed in their jobs which they find stimulating, challenging, and remunerative. They buy a charming house on the outskirts of the city and in due course have two beautiful children to whom they are fully devoted. On weekends the four of them go on picnics and together take fun vacations overseas.

The children grow up to be decent, law abiding citizens, making their parents very proud.

Eventually Dr. Robert and Mary Livingston die and move to a room "in My Father's house" (John 14:2) and live happily ever after.

Jonathan meets Eva in a pub. Eva falls head over heels in love with Jonathan. Jonathan, however, is not that crazy about her. He uses her for his selfish pleasure and ego gratification, nothing more. Eva is hopeful that should she continue to do his biddings and satisfy his needs, he will come around. Jonathan visits Eva twice a week on fixed days with soiled clothes which she washes and presses for him. Eva cooks him dinner and after toying with her for a while falls asleep while Eva does the dirty dishes. While Jonathan is asleep Eva puts on fresh lip stick, does her hair, and makes a strenuous effort to look good when he wakes up. He, however, takes no notice of her; he just walks out of the house.

On one visit Jonathan complains about the food which he has never done before. Eva is very hurt and with effort refrains from crying as crying would harm her appearance.

Friends at Eva's office notice that she is constantly downcast and moody, they tell her Jonathan is a rat and a scoundrel and that she should kick him out. Eva persists. She is hopeful. She loves him dearly. She believes there is a good Jonathan inside the Jonathan she sees twice a week. She is convinced this other good, invisible Jonathan will emerge like a butterfly from a cocoon, like a Jack from a box, a pit from a prune, if only she is patient.

Until one day:

Eva's friends tell her they regularly see Jonathan with another woman, having meals in a restaurant. Eva is terribly depressed, devastated in fact. Jonathan has not once taken her out to a restaurant. Eva takes all the sleeping pills and aspirin in her medicine cabinet and, leaving a note for Jonathan, downs it with a shot of Vodka.

She hopes Jonathan will discover the note, rush her to the hospital in time, and she will be saved. Jonathan will repent, and thereafter they will be together for ever.

This does not happen. Eva dies. Jonathan is now married to that other woman whom Eva's friends saw at the restaurant.

Neil meets Mary at work and falls in love with her. Even though she sleeps with him, she is not in love with him. She's in love with James who is not ready to settle down. James is often out with his buddies on his motorcycle and fast cars. He reserves Thursdays for Mary. This is the only day he can get away from his buddies. Mary does not mind. She's sure he will settle down with her.

One day, not a Thursday, James breezes in on his motorcycle with a top- grade California wine. They get stoned and get into bed. Neil who has a key to the apartment is completely surprised. She takes out his gun and shoots James, Mary and himself. All three are rushed to the hospital. Mary alone survives.

After a respectable period of mourning Mary marries Alfred, a home bird she met at a church fair. They have three lovely children. Weekends they go on picnics and together take fun vacations overseas.

37

Compliment Conundrum

I attended what no one will dispute is the best girl's high school in my country. I always compare this high school to Choate in Connecticut where I live now. At end of term I would carry away many prizes. There was just one medical college in my country at this time. Thousands compete for admission for the few vacancies. You can say "many are called, very few are chosen."

I always wanted to be a doctor as it had prestige; and doctors, I observed, end up well-heeled. I was selected and I qualified as a doctor. From here I proceeded to the United Kingdom and specialized in neurology. In pediatric neurology, to be precise.

Afterward I migrated to the United States. I married a talented attorney (now why this choice - because I feared malpractice lawsuits) who had a very lucrative practice. I am, "if I may say so in all humility," well known in all of New England. Our two children--a boy and a girl--attend Yale and Harvard. My husband's and my work and our responsibilities to our children allowed very little time for fun.

It's about time I ride on the crest of my fortune and fame, I thought. I wanted to meet my friends from the old and give them an opportunity to see for themselves what a success I have made of myself. Every year during summer there is a reunion dinner. I have never attended this. This year I am going to.

I wanted to look my best. I made several visits to Neiman Marcus and finally found a dress I really liked. I do not shop during sale time. It's my belief that only what the shop wants to get rid of is put on "sale." I found a beautiful Ivanka creation (I do not subscribe to her father's political views, though) and the usual accoutrements to match.

I waited anxiously for the day, which finally arrived. Cocktails at 6 and dinner at 7 P.M. at the Waldorf, the invitation read. Word had got around I would be attending, and the chief organizer was being bombarded with requests for an introduction. So said the chief organizer, making a special call to me.

I was not going to arrive sharp at 6.00 like the rest of the crowd. I will walk in at 6.30 when most, if not all, of the guests would be on their feet. I would then make a dramatic entry, causing all heads to turn in my direction. I swanned in at half past six, dressed to the nines. On seeing me the chief organizer hurried towards me, all heads turned in my direction, and there was haunted silence. As soon as she got close to me, extending her hand, she said, "What a pretty dress." I did not offer my hand. Like a statue nailed to the floor I remained fixed on the spot. Then I shrugged my shoulders, shook my head, cast up my eyes, but said nothing.

The chief organizer then asked, "Are you O.K.?" I did not answer. I heard some of the guests remark, "She's weird."

I was certain the dress would evoke admiring comments. For months I had given thought, very serious thought to how gracefully I should respond.

I would say, "My daughter picked this for me."

"I bought it on sale."

"You really think so."

"I like your outfit too."

"Oh no, this is so old I was about to donate it to Goodwill."

"I feel like a hobo in this august gathering."

Not one of these came to my mind.

How true the sages are - "You don't get a second chance to make a first impression."

38

The getaway Car

After a full day of Christmas shopping at a mall and loaded with parcels, a woman returned to the parking lot just in time to see a man climb into her brand-new Ford Lincoln.

"Stop!" she cried. "Get away from that car. You thief!"

The man looked at her with unvarnished contempt.

"Get out of my way, lady. Who do you think you are?"

The angry woman dropped her shopping bags, opened her purse, and took out a hand gun.

"Get out of the car soon or I'll shoot" she said.

"You're out of your mind, silly lady," the man said as he climbed out of the car and started to walk toward the woman. Before she knew what, she pulled the trigger and shot the man in the leg.

"You are insane," the man screamed; and clutching his wounded leg, he dragged himself away and hid below one of the neighboring cars.

Frightened that she would be arrested, the woman threw all her packages into the back seat of the car and climbed in behind the steering wheel for a quick getaway. This is when she realized this was not her car.

39

Amin's choice

In a remote village in Uganda in the seventies a woman began to go into labor. The nearest doctor was in a town several miles away. While the mother did what she could to assist, the husband rushed off to summon a doctor.

A few hours later, the husband and the doctor arrived at the house to find the woman had given birth to twins--a boy and a girl. They were very small, of extremely low birth weight, and they had turned blue.

The doctor sat down beside the mother.

"Mrs. Amin" the doctor said, "the babies need oxygen urgently, but I only have in my medical bag enough to save one of the children. I must ask you to choose."

The new mother wept and kissed her two babies. Then she handed over one of the tiny infants to the doctor.

"Here, doctor" said the mother, picking up the boy. "Save my little Idi."

Idi Amin—who later was feared for the atrocities he committed on his own people.

40

The package of cookies

A New York woman was early for her train home so she stepped into a coffee shop, ordered a cappuccino, and bought a small package of cookies.

All the tables in the café were occupied. But there was one vacant seat at a small table at which a well- dressed man was seated reading a newspaper.

"There are no other vacant seats, sir" the woman pleaded. "Do you mind if I join you?"

"Not at all, be my guest," the man said with a smile and went back to reading his newspaper. He paid no attention to the woman until she opened her package of cookies. He folded his newspaper and set it on the table beside his coffee.

The woman took a cookie from the package. Without saying a word, the man also took a cookie from the package. The woman took another cookie from the package, and the man did the same.

The woman was utterly speechless. She had never seen such effrontery.

She stared at the man as he took one more. He returned the stare and took another. This went on for quite a while.

Finally, when there was only one cookie left, the man picked it up, broke it into two, and offered half to the woman.

"Please, madam, I insist," he said.

The woman at this point lost her self-control.

"You insist! The cheek! You help yourself to my food and then try to make a gallant gesture! You are the most insufferable oaf I've ever met!"

"I'm insufferable?" the man shouted back. "Who do you think opened my package of cookies and began to eat them?"

"No one," the woman cried. "Look! Your package of cookies is still sitting there unopened on your brief case."

41

The Juju Man

It happened in Monrovia in the West African nation of Liberia. I was employed as a controller for a construction company engaged in World Bank projects.

At a certain time during my sojourn with the company strange things began to happen. Every Monday morning when we reported for work, items of small value were found to be missing. The value of items began getting bigger and bigger as the Mondays rolled by, from pocket calculators to heavy adding machines. It soon reached the point that it became a guessing game as to what would be missing next. Men and women would discuss the robbery in whispers in corners. There were no signs ever of a break in. Even without the help of Sherlock Holmes we all knew it must be an inside job.

It was a Saturday, around eleven thirty in the morning. The closing time was twelve noon. I observed men and women running down the stairs making a loud noise. I followed the sound and found myself in the yard adjoining the main office. A circle had formed. In the center squatted a man, unkempt, gaunt, with a face resembling a battle axe, dressed in African garb on which time had left her grisly marks, indicating the supercilious, imperious comportment of a Liberian cop.

He had a rusty basin with yellow liquid, a machete, and some leaves. On inquiry I was informed he was a Juju man and had been sent for by the president. His job was to identify the thief. The president too was present.

The Juju man proceeded to call those present to come one by one and take the test. He would request the participant to hold one end of the machete while he held the other. He placed some leaves on the machete and sprinkled the yellow liquid from the basin. The one being tested was then asked to loosen his grip on the machete and withdraw his hand. A guilty person would not be able to let go of the machete, we were told. Everyone present passed the test. I was not called. I teetered towards volunteering for the experience but backed off. I had no faith in this addled, arcane art of detection and feared of being implicated.

What bewildered me more was that in the circle of participants were members of the staff who were sophisticated, skilled professionals, educated and trained in the United States, very western in their ways, who were readily submitting themselves to the dictates of a Juju man and unquestioningly awaiting the outcome.

At this point, someone in the group asked, "Where's Alfred?" He's in the office working on the payroll came the reply. "Send for him," the president ordered. Alfred Koroma, a Sierra Leonean, was always the first to arrive and last to leave the office. Reticent, intractable, always with a tortured expression, he kept mostly to himself.

Alfred arrived. He had that perplexed "what is this all about" look. He was asked to submit to the now familiar routine.

Alfred held the machete at one end and the Juju man the other. Leaves were placed and the yellow liquid sprinkled as before. The Juju man now asked Alfred Koroma to loosen his grip on the machete and remove his hand. He could not. He tried very hard. A gasp escaped from the crowd and then total silence.

The Juju man lapsed into an incantation lasting about a minute or two at the end of which Alfred was able to let go of the machete. Alfred got testy. He remonstrated that the whole exercise was a farce and should not be relied upon.

The Juju man with unflappable demeanor asked Alfred, "Are you challenging me?" Alfred hesitated and then with a hang-dog expression replied between clenched teeth, "NO!" and made a dash for his cubicle faster than a discharged bullet.

It is believed that had Alfred challenged the veracity of this test, the Juju man could cast a spell and some harm would come to him before sunset.

The president was a witness to all this. He returned to his office, his head bowed with the anguish that takes hold of a jockey when agonizing whether or not to shoot his injured horse. He said nary a word. Alfred was his favorite, his pride, his pick of the litter.

Alfred Koroma was not fired. He was not called upon to pay for the stolen property. He was not admonished. The robberies stopped, and Mondays resumed their uneventful monotony once more.

"There are more things in heaven and earth, Horatio, than are dreamt of in your philosophy." Hamlet

42

The Well-Dress Thief

A 19 year-old kid lived with his parents and went to college near their house. One night, while his mother and father were out of town, the kid worked until eleven o'clock at the college library. As he walked across the nearly deserted parking lot, someone grabbed him from behind and held a gun to his head.

"Get in your car, drive me to your house, and you won't get hurt," the gunman said.

The boy was frightened so he did what he was told. At the house the thief ordered the boy into the cellar, tied him up, gagged him, and then went back upstairs. For the next hour, the boy lay helplessly in the cellar, listening to the robber ransack the house.

The next morning the boy's parents returned. The thief had stolen computers, televisions, stereo systems, jewelry, silverware, and the boy's prize possession – his Versace sweater.

A week later, the police called the family to announce that they had arrested the suspect. They wanted the kid to come down to the station and identify the thief in a line-up.

When the boy looked through the glass, he recognized the thief immediately.

"That's him," he told the detective. "The second on the right.

"That was fast, son," the detective said. "How can you be so sure?"

"Because he is wearing my sweater."

43

How I arrived at the supermarket

One hot day in June I slipped into New York harbor aboard the S.S. Samaria, flying the Liberian flag, having traveled in a container some three thousand miles from Ecuador. I traveled through the Panama Canal along with cargo from the Caribbean in the company of spiders, snakes, chirping crickets, cockroaches and many other creepy, crawly creatures I could not identify.

At Brooklyn when the hatch was opened for inspection, stowaways who were physically close to me jumped out and took to their heels, I know not whither.

From Brooklyn where I was given a once over by customs officials who discarded some of my close traveling friends. On a second journey I traveled in a large loop around the city, and finally I was taken away in an unmarked truck by night.

We were inspected by United States customs officials and border protection. We were inspected by men wearing short-sleeved green shirts with the company name on the breast pocket

Here several well-dressed men, having arrived in expensive cars, began bidding for us. Reminded me of past slave auctions. Before the bidding began, some caressed us and some pinched or poked us. Thereafter a few of us were put in a container and taken by truck to a place I now know to be Connecticut.

In America I am in demand more than oranges and apples combined.

Not many are aware of this. Evidence from ancient translations of the Bible suggest that it was not an apple that was forbidden. It was I. I appear in corporate board rooms and in kitchens everywhere. Sad to say, I may not last long. My days are numbered. I have become so frail I am now susceptible to blights and pestilence.

Here I am now in a supermarket with customers again pinching, prodding and poking me all the time. I hear them say "too ripe" or "too green," "too yellow" or "hard as hammers."

I cause injuries whenever they merely step on me. How mean, I think. Those of us who were disease resistant are in great demand. We had to be careful. If one got sick all got sick.

I am called by different names – "Belinda," "Bonita," "Del Monte," "Chiquita," "Dole," and many more. But to my creator I will always be "Top Banana" although of late the Avocado has been challenging my preeminence. "I shall overcome."

44

Threesome

Seated in the living room, Troika was gazing fondly, nostalgically at the three children playing and teasing and cavorting. At the far end of the room was Troika's mother. She was granny and nanny to the kids, whom she loved dearly.

Troika's three children, all boys, were by three different men.

The first was African, the father a Sierra Leonean named Banya.

The second was Indian, a Sikh whose father's name was Harjan Singh.

The third French, Mitterand was the father' name.

Each child retained the father's last name. This presented certain difficulties when registering them at school. It raised eye brows. Troika remembered their fathers so fondly it never bothered her. In fact, she would spend hours looking at their pictures.

Troika was keen the children should continue to observe their family heritage. Each child inherited a different cultural trait from his father. Banya, African generosity; Harjan Singh, the Indian Sikh, with unpruned long hair, which was a religious requirement, paid close attention to his studies; and the French Mitterand enjoyed the company of girls.

Troika begat them when she worked as a clerk in the Indian embassy abroad.

Troika liked this variety, this symphony, this melodious ensemble.

It was like having her past fresh, running around the house. It was like having all the variety concentrated in one place.

Troika had her good and not so good moments. The boys developed normally, unperturbed by the ghosts of their mother's past. She kept paternity as far as possible from the children, nudging them ever closer to herself.

When Troika saw each of her children's faces, her thoughts fling back to each of their fathers and the happy, very enjoyable times she had with each of them.

Looking at Banya, memories of Freetown came to her, the Atlantic Ocean caressing the hills, the leisurely walks along Lumley beach, fishermen setting out in their canoes at the crack of dawn.

Harjan Singh, the majestic Taj Mahal in Agra, the imposing Red Fort in New Delhi, the Brindavan Gardens of Bangalore.

Mitterand, the Eiffel Tower, the Versailles Palace, which was not equipped with a toilet, the parties, the parks, the trip to the Art Gallery to view the inscrutable smile of the Mona Lisa.

There was a time when Troika was young, attractive, vivacious, and desirable.

What a shame the old order must change to yield place to the new. Nobody wants her now. She longs for the past. Seldom does she go out on a date; and when she does, she omits reference to her sons. Taking them anywhere prompts too many questions. Each day the boys are spending more time with Troika's mother and less with her.

She sorely misses having a man in the house, one with whom she could freely and without fear discuss finances, the children's health, and the children's future.

She is resigned. "Everything is going to be fine," she says confidently, "with the kind of mother I have."

45

Yoga and Savi

Yoga and Savi in short boy-cut hair could be seen walking in the evenings around the block hand in hand, chatting companionly, engaged in mordant marital banter. All those living in the condominium complex admired the couple's amorous ways, their fondness for each other. They were a very friendly couple and would always smile and exchange pleasantries with the neighbors.

It was well known to friends and family and those in the complex that Savi was afflicted with a heart condition.

Yoga's dear friend Luke came to know that Yoga was one of the victims in the Las Vegas shooting. It was going to be extremely difficult to break the sad news to Savi.

Luke rushed over to Savi's house to covey the news, and there he met Savi's sister Rohini. It was now Rohini's job to break the crushing news to Savi.

In broken sentences, veiled hints, Rohini informed Savi of her husband's death while Luke stood by.

To most women the news would have given a knock-out blow. Not so with Savi. Stoically, she took the blow on the chin and then fell into the outstretched arms of her sister and wept. When the storm of grief had spent itself, when she was able to rein in her emotions, Savi went away into her room alone, thoughtfully, mournfully. She permitted no one into her room.

Kneeling at the bed facing an open window, she let the news sink into her soul. It was a fine day. She could see the open square before her house and the tops of trees that were springing to life. She could hear the cavorting of birds and bees, the happy banter of children, and peddlers hawking their wares in competition.

She knelt in silence. Except for an occasional sob which escaped and interrupted her thoughts, she was at peace.

She was a college graduate, young, intelligent and very attractive. Her husband who had been very protective and possessive prohibited her from going out to work.

She now felt a change come over her. She did not resist it. Instead she surrendered to this feeling creeping in her insides. She heard herself saying over and over under her breath, involuntarily, "Free! Free! Free Forever"

"Afoot and lighthearted I take to the open road,

Healthy, free, the world before me,

The long brown path before me,

Leading wherever, I choose."

The vacant stare and look of terror that had followed her into the room disappeared from her eyes. Was it a kind of monstrous joy that lay dormant all these years now stirring to life? She knew very well she would weep once more when she saw the kind and tender hands of her husband folded in death. She knew well that as time passed, she would tearfully recall their happy times

And yet, yet, she was determined to see beyond this "reversal of fortune." It was only yesterday she was depressed that life was tediously long. She was now, with a fancy running riot, looking forward to happy days, happy spring days and happy summer days. Being a voracious reader, she was familiar with Steinbeck's famous words in <u>Travels with Charlie</u>: "What good is the warmth of summer if not for the cold of winter to give it sweetness."

Yes. Savi was set to enjoy the warmth of summer days to come, having spent until now the cold of winter.

While she was thus blissfully contemplating the days ahead, she heard her sister who was kneeling before the closed door, begging for admission. "Savi, open the door! I beg, open the door. You'll make yourself ill, Savi. For heaven's sake, open the door."

Savi arose and opened the door, submitting to her sister's importunities.

Clasping her sister's waist, like a Goddess of Victory, they both lumbered down the stairs. Luke stood waiting for them at the bottom.

Everyone heard the pitiless click of the dead bolt as he unlocked the door. There was Yoga with briefcase in hand, travel stained and famished. He had been far from the place of the shooting. He had heard about it and rushed home to be with his wife.

Savi let out a piercing scream and fell to the floor.

When the doctor came, he pronounced her dead, having died of heart disease.

46

Mind over Matters that May or May not Matter

I t has been said it is not violence but silence that kills a marriage. Silence, some feel, is violence.

One really wonders. Take for instance Mr. Freddie and Mrs. Fannie Sitput. They have been married for years, double the total of your fingers and toes together and yet you'll still fall short by a toe or two.

Over the years, while they sipped their morning coffee, this couple slipped into a state in which there was no need for spontaneous, sustained, audible conversation.

A word, a comment, a smile, a sour face, a casual remark from one, and the two minds, Freddie and Fannie's minds in tandem, would take over from there on, just the way the hybrid Toyota engages from gasoline to battery with fluid ease and back to gasoline without a fuss, nary a pause.

While Freddie and Fannie's bodies sat in pregnant silence, their two minds would aggressively argue, dissent, agree and disagree. "Time Out!" one mind would say to the other. "Let's defer this for another day."

Just then there would be another innocuous comment, "Wonder whether it's going to rain today," and right away the two minds would once again be locked in conference, in hand-to-hand combat, and after a few cartwheels and calisthenics there would be a meeting of the two minds.

Any spectator watching these two, Buddha-like, bodies in stasis with minds in perpetual motion, would be deceived.

"Look at them," someone might comment. "They barely talk."

Little would the spectator suspect that the couple is exhausted beyond words – their minds have traveled up and down, back and forth and in circles, covering politics, parenting, children, grandchildren, the work place highs and lows, and much more.

Little do these neophytes realize that the minds of this couple over scores of years and more have plumbed each other's souls so thoroughly and for so long that their reactions have become as predictable and real as their punctuated heavy breathing and perennial coughing. Like the almost denuded forest of the Amazon or the diminishing oil reserve of Saudi Arabia, there is little now left to be tapped.

Freddie pushes his chair back, empty coffee cup in hand…

Fannie remarks, "I suppose you are going to the patio to smoke your cigar." "I'll soon join you," she says.

For this couple few words are enough to cement their mutual understanding, appreciation, and connubial bliss.

47

How I Replaced my Car's Hub Cap

In the early sixties, where I come from, a person bought his first second-hand car (meaning pre-owned) only after he landed his first job with a salary sufficient to pay for spare parts and petrol. The car enjoyed a privileged position among a person's total assets. On the status totem-pole you were up there. Spit polished and hand washed, the car would be shining in the tropical sun year-round. All cars are garaged and bolted overnight.

I bought my first car, a second- hand Wolsey 1300, after I got a job as an accountant. I was very proud of this car. One day when I came up to my car from a spot of shopping in the Fort area, I noticed one hub cap missing. I was very upset. A new hub cap cost a tidy sum in those days when importation of cars and parts was restricted. A friend found a way to replace the hub cap. There's always a way.

He tells me to go to this place called Panchikawatte, which is about five miles from my home, and inquire in one of a row of shops, tiny boutiques really, and they are sure to help. I have never been to this part of the city before. Never had the stones to visit any joint which I felt might be seedy.

So around noon on a Saturday I set out for Panchikawatte. I was nervous. I had a sneaky feeling it was not legit. Anyway, I went to this place and looked into the various shops. In almost all of them the man who looked like the proprietor was very busy transacting business.

But there was one where the owner was just reading the newspapers. I explained to him in faltering, ungrammatical Sinhala that I needed a hub cap. "Let me see," he says. So, the two of us and a little boy go up to my car. I show him the replacement cap I needed. *It was right rear.*

"Fine, let's go back to the shop," he says, and all three of us trudge to his boutique. He then tells the young fella "Martin, Mahathaya (Master) needs a hub cap; go get one quick." I think that's what he must have said. I could see the boy open a drawer, pick up a screw driver and set off. The whole thing didn't look kosher to me at all.

After sitting nervously waiting, Martin came back with a hub cap. The owner hurriedly gave me the hub cap wrapped in a newspaper, took ten rupees for it, and sent me off. With mixed feelings of guilt and satisfaction I hurriedly returned home. I parked the car at home, went around to open the boot to remove my belongings.

The *left rear* hub cap was missing!

48

The Stereo

Peter's father left his mother a few months after he was born – they never heard from him again. Peter's mother had barely finished high school. She managed to get a job as a filing clerk in a lawyer's office; she worked two and three jobs and on weekends too. She saw first-hand and admired the work the attorneys were doing. She wanted Peter to become an attorney at all costs. "Peter will have the best, the very best, I can afford," she vowed.

Peter was now thirteen years-old. Peter's friends had Sanyo and Philips stereos with detachable speakers. On Friday nights he would visit these friends and listen avidly to the music. He would come home and describe to his mother in detail the grand time he had.

On his next birthday Peter's mother surprised him with a mini stereo with detachable speakers, the same kind his friends had. Peter was ecstatic. On Fridays he would now invite his friends to his house, and with the music turned up full blast they danced till dawn.

On another Friday night eight weeks later, when he, his friends, and their girlfriends were having a rollicking time at Peter's house, there was a knock on the front door. Funny, he thought. The knock got louder. Peter opened the door to find two men.

One was the proprietor of the department store where the stereo had been bought and the other a cop. They retrieved the mini stereo right in the presence of his friends. His mother could not keep up with the payments, it appears. She was very much in arrears. Peter was humiliated. He could not believe what had happened to him. How could this happen to me? Why me? He could not forgive his mother.

The next morning very early, Peter saw his mother go to work, come home in the evening, and then go out to her next job. She had never been on a vacation, never entertained, and politely turned down dinner invitations because she could not reciprocate.

Twenty years later:

Peter is now an attorney, senior partner, in a leading law firm in New York City.

In his large house Peter is entertaining his friends, twenty couples in all. There is music and dancing and such an abundance of food, served by liveried waiters, that it would even embarrass Caligula. Peter was in fine fettle. His twelve- year-old daughter approaches her father and says, "Dad, grandma is crying."

Peter rushes to his mother, now in her eighties. As he obediently stands in front of his mother, his thoughts flash back to the day there was a knock on the door.

49

Dreading Wednesdays

Josephine Lokubadah was eighty-five years-old. Her husband, to whom she was married for sixty -five years, had died. She had lived in this house in New Jersey all her married life. She had two daughters, Ganja and Beedi. Ganjah, the older of the two, lived with her family in San Francisco. Beedi lived with hers in Chicago.

The New Jersey house, though commodious and well-appointed, stirred memories that further compounded the sadness of her loss. She did not to wish to live in this house any longer. Josephine Lokubadah owned a small house, free of encumbrances, in the quiet village of Shanksville in Pennsylvania. The house was situated very close to the quiet, friendly homes of Amish families. Only the sound of the horse and trap separated her house from the good Amish folks. Josephine Lokubadah was convinced the tranquility of the Amish surroundings was ideal for her troubled and undulating emotional state.

Although feeble of body, she was firm of resolve. The house in Shanksville had not been lived in for many years. She had it repaired and refurbished. It had a large bed room with attached bath and a spare room on the upper floor. The kitchen was on the ground floor. The finished basement had a half bath. The movers came in and transported items that she would need in her new dwelling. The bed and books went into the large room; the exercise bicycle, television, VCR, and the small refrigerator in which she always had Coke, cheese, and chocolate, went into the basement.

She moved into her new dwelling on Sunday morning, with groceries to last a week. Everything was left just where the movers had deposited them. Josephine Lokubadah had neither the desire nor the inclination to make new friends. She was going to live the life of a recluse. So long as she could find a competent, friendly doctor, she felt self-sufficient.

Her life fell into a placid pattern. She remained confined indoors. Once a week she would set out in her elegant Saturn car to the supermarket for groceries. She always had an early meal, telephoned daughters Ganjah and Beedi to inform them she was doing fine, and retired to her bedroom. She bolted the bedroom door. She had all her requirements in her bedroom. Once in her bedroom she would not leave until daybreak when she felt safe to do so.

The peace and quiet she longed for and enjoyed was not to last. One night she thought there were sounds coming from the basement. She pulled the covers over her head and went to sleep. The next morning, she found everything in its place. It must be my imagination, she mused, and went about her work. The following week she heard the sounds again. Loud screams and gun shots in muffled tones were heard through the chinks in the door.

She did not inform the children. She was afraid though. She chanted several mantras in the basement and burned incense sticks to drive away the evil spirits. The weird sounds continued. She left offerings of chocolate and chewing gum to assuage the stubborn spirits. The evil intruders could not be appeased.

"Haunted! Haunted! This house is haunted," she moaned. Visions of incubus, goblins, and gnomes crashed through her frail mind. It occurred to her now that the sounds were heard only on Wednesday nights. She was too frightened to check the time. She began to dread Wednesdays. The passing of each day meant a day closer to Wednesday. She lost her appetite. She became a bundle of twisted nerves. She could not face this fear singly any longer. She called Ganja and Beedi and wailed, "I'm 85, I am a widow, and I'm afraid."

Ganjah in San Francisco mentioned it to her husband Luke who replied, "Your mother is going bonkers." At the same time in Chicago Harry was telling his wife Beedi, "Your mother is going bonkers." The sisters conferred. The four of them talked it over on a conference call. It was decided that their mother should admit herself into a Senior Home where she would have company and constant care.

"Leave me out of this," the husbands Luke and Harry protested in unison.

Who would make the suggestion to the mother? Neither Ganjah nor Beedi volunteered. One does not volunteer to twirl the whiskers of a tiger. Since there were no volunteers, it was agreed that whichever daughter got the first call on Thursday should patiently hear her mother out, count to ten, and then suggest she should call the police as soon as she hears those noises.

Ganjah and Beedi throughout the week reminded themselves continuously, "Be patient, Be patient with Ma, Count to ten."

Wednesday night Josephine Lokubadah heard those noises again. She felt she was coming apart. She could converse fluently in English, Italian, Spanish and French. She prayed in all four. The harrowing sounds, though seemingly endless, usually lasted two hours. She prayed as never before that it would soon be over. She heard someone moving up and down the stairs. And then, as always, there was silence.

Ganjah's telephone rang in the morning. She knew it was her mother. The mother began, "You know, daughter." But before she could complete the sentence, Ganjah cut her off, "You should call the local police. That's what they are there for." The conversation exploded in midsentence, killed in the crib. Ganjah immediately regretted what she had said. This is not how she wanted it to come out. Her mother fell silent. She whispered, "Maybe I should call the police. Where the mantras have failed the might of the police may succeed." Sadly, she placed the receiver in the telephone cradle.

That whole week Mrs. Lokubadah devoted herself to memorizing the telephone number of the local police. If you had wished her "Good Morning," she would have replied with the police number. She thought of nothing else. As sure as Wednesday would come, she heard the noises. Stretching her hand out from under the covers, she lifted the telephone and punched the numbers. "I am 85 years old. I am a widow and I am afraid. Come immediately," she pleaded. The police promised they would be there in under ten minutes.

No one came and she passed the time in agony and prayer. The next morning, she directed the call to Beedi. Beedi had been forewarned by her sister of her own disastrous performance. Beedi listened to everything her mother had to say, counted to twenty, and replied, "You are a law-abiding citizen, Ma. You pay your taxes. Complain to the officer in charge of the precinct." Her mother agreed .

The officer on duty who took the call referred to the notes and replied, "Madam, a police car was sent. The officer found No 8 Windy Street quiet; and as he cannot enter the premises without a search warrant or an invitation from the principal occupant, he had to return."

Mrs. Lokubadah informed the officer she lived in No. 18 and not No. 8 Windy Street. "You have my permission to enter my house using whatever means are necessary."

The officer made his notes and, mildly amused, informed his colleagues. He had a grandmother of the same age. The call did come on Wednesday night. It was around half past nine. There was nothing exciting going on that night. Four officers, two in mufti and two in uniform, armed and wearing bullet proof vests, set out in two cars for 18 Windy Street. They parked the cars a distance away from the house. The two in mufti stayed by the cars while the uniformed two, treading very softly, stealthily made their way to No 18, fingers on the triggers and in crouched position prepared for any emergency. While on the drive way they heard faint sounds filtering from the basement.

They let themselves in by picking the front door lock and went to the basement. It was dark. An officer turned on the lights. Both officers fell to the floor and shouted "POLICE." They had come prepared for a shootout. What they saw surprised them. They called out, "Mrs. Lokubadah, it's safe to come down now."

Mrs. Lokubadah came down to the basement. Tears welled up in her eyes. Seated in a large chair were two children no more than 8 years of age. There was an opened can of coke on the floor and crumbs of cheese on the children's faces. They had fallen asleep in a seated position. On the television screen, a Harry Potter DVD tape was playing. The children, frightened at the sight of the police, began crying. They said that because they were Amish, they had no television in their home and were not allowed to watch movies. On Wednesday nights the parents had an Amish night of prayer and meditation from 8 o'clock to well past midnight. They borrowed tapes from friends and watched them in Mrs. Lokubadah's basement. They were brother and sister. They pleaded with the police not to mention this to their parents. The punishment would be severe.

One officer said, "O.K., let's make a deal. We will not inform your parents if you agree not to come to this house or any other house without your parents' permission."

"We will not come again, sir," the children pledged. Mrs. Lokubadah was viewing all this with sympathy and amusement.

"Now," said one officer, "Let's see how you get out." They heaved and pulled aside the large chair in which they had fallen asleep. Behind the chair was a small trap door leading to the garden. Mrs. Lokubadah had not given any thought to this door. The chair had been carelessly placed by the movers, and she had not made any changes, so it remained that way. The children knew every corner and crevice in the house. They used to play in it for long hours when the house was unoccupied.

Two weeks later at the supermarket Mrs. Lokubadah saw the two children. They recognized her. They exchanged smiles and moved on. Mrs. Lokubadah was puzzled. "What are they up to this time?" she wondered.

She was aware Amish children, even adults for that matter, did not shop at supermarkets. She quickly moved to the next aisle, picked up a can of soup, and turned back. A rueful expression lingered across the freckled face of this forlorn, frightened dowager.

Ruminating over her experiences of the past few weeks, Mrs. Lokubadah followed the children with her eyes until they were lost in the crush of shoppers.

Her sleep was no longer interrupted. She lived to be a hundred.

50

The wages of war

P am and Tony have a son, four years old. Tony is in the army and was sent to Fallujah. Ever since he left for Fallujah, Pam dreaded she may be in for bad news. In the kitchen while making breakfast for her son, she keeps looking through the window, praying she will not see the army messenger walking to her home. For each day of no news she is thankful.

On a sunny day in May from the kitchen window she sees a young soldier in starched khaki shirt, meticulously clean shaven and upright, walk towards her house and is now on her driveway.

"O God, please let it be a mistake. The wrong house, please." The doorbell rings, and Pam pleads with her mother, "Don't open the door." She thinks, "We'll pretend we are not here. We'll not get the news, and everything will be fine." Her mother, although moved by her daughter's anguish, knows, however, that she has to let the messenger in.

Pam does not remember much of the conversation. Something about Tony going in search of a fellow soldier having been ambushed. The man says everything that he has been trained to say. Tony was a daring soldier who gave his life for his country and so forth. He speaks to Pam's mother since Pam does not make eye contact with the soldier. Looking down on Pam's son, he says, "He's got every reason to be proud of his dad," and leaves.

At the cemetery fifty or so people gather around a trench as two well-dressed soldiers fold an American flag into a perfect triangle and hand it to Pam, while her son holds tightly to his mother's dress.

The story of Tony's death is on the seven o'clock news. A head shot of Tony in khaki flashes across the screen. There is a short clip of Pam, her mother, and Tony's parents sitting in her living room. The reporter asks the questions she has asked a thousand times before.

"How are you dealing with this? Did you ever expect this to happen? What are your feelings on the war?" She turns around to Tony's mother and says, "Remember, your son did not die in vain. He volunteered to go looking for his friend. He died for his country."

The anchor woman moves on to make room for a commercial.

Friends from distant places call. Neighbors drop by. All speak in praise of Tony's self-sacrifice.

The army never disclosed that Tony died in friendly fire.

51

Fake News

Christopher Columbus couldn't discover America because he did not have a valid visa.

The Mayflower pilgrims were not allowed to land. The immigration quotas were full.

It was Tenzing Norgay who was the first to reach the peak of Mt. Everest. Edmund Hillary joined him later. The BBC altered the names.

The Titanic did arrive in New York without any problem. This was suppressed on the instructions of the film makers.

Neal Armstrong actually landed on a little island in the Caribbean called "Moon."

Princes Diana did not die in the car crash. The accident was staged. Dodi Al-Fayed and Princess Diana now live incognito in a tiny village in North Korea.

David knocked out Goliath with his fifth stone, not his first.

52

Budget Blues

In 1972 responding to numerous complaints Doug Seneviratne was sent by the World Health Organization to visit a distant village hospital in Bo in Sierra Leone in West Africa and report on conditions there. After great difficulty cutting through dense bushes, he barely managed to elbow his way through and arrived at the hospital.

On arrival he asked to speak with the office manager. He wasn't in. He then asked to see the chief of medical services and was told he was out to lunch. After two hours of waiting the chief turned up.

Dr. Seneviratne saw patients dying, spitting up blood, and many more were burning with fever while covered in sores with flies buzzing all over.

There was not a single doctor in sight. When Dr. Seneviratne inquired where all the doctors were, the chief of medical services explained thus:

"The doctors come in only when the nurses call them."

Losing his cool somewhat, he asked, "So why don't the nurses call the doctors?"

"We don't have the budget for nurses," replied the chief of medical services.

53

Ash to Ashes

Yielding to years of persistent public pressure in the principality of Liechtenstein, which connects Switzerland and Austria like a hyphen, the government finally concluded that a firing squad as a way of putting criminals to death was barbaric, and to the relief of many it was abandoned. The government decided the inhumane gallows and hooded executioner, too, should be done away with.

Civilization, the authorities felt, demanded an immediate, scientific, foolproof, and pain-free death. This news was hailed by all.

The first prisoner after the new law was enacted was going to be put to death in public so that it would be known to all that executions were being carried out according to the new law.

A large gathering of sightseers had gathered in an open-air stadium to witness the execution. It was being televised. All the channels carried it, at home and abroad.

To ensure instant death, the prisoner, gagged and bound with heavy belts, received a three-hundred volt shock. He writhed and moaned, but alas, after all the precautions and pious intentions, he did not die.

They cranked up the generator and passed four hundred volts through him. More violent spasms, but still alive.

The public was in complete disbelief. Calls of protest from all over the world were bombarding the Liechtenstein government.

The authorities now decided on a "do or die" approach.

They administered seven hundred volts.

His snout exploded in a spurt of foaming blood, and to the horror of the witnessing public and the shame of the Liechtenstein government, a throaty ear- piercing howl was heard by all.

The fourth shot finally did him in.

He had been convicted summarily without a trial, purely on hearsay evidence.

Sadly, it transpired that it was a case of mistaken identity. It was his identical twin brother Smash who committed the crime.

The crime?

Biting two children in the street.

The dog's name was Ash.

54

Blinds sighted

A woman had just undressed and was about to step into the shower when she heard the doorbell ring.

"Who is it?" she shouted from the bathroom window.

"Blind man," a man answered.

The woman sighed. It was too much trouble to get dressed again, so she thought she would run downstairs and hand the poor man some money as she was.

"There's nothing to be ashamed of," she told herself. "He can't see a thing. Blind man didn't he say?"

The naked woman grabbed a few dollars from her purse and threw open the door.

The man on the back porch gasped. Then he laughed.

"Where would you like me to hang the blinds eh….eh… madam?"

55

Three's no company

The children have married and left. They have their own children to worry about. One would think the old couple would now be experiencing the proverbial empty nest syndrome. Just the two of them. Bored stiff! Not so.

There was a third person now in the house. He came uninvited and is determined to stay. We refer to this person as "He," but we do not know if it's a He or a She.

Like a child who is always hungry, He demanded attention constantly. He woke up the old couple in the dead of night and refused to go to sleep. He sat up in the big chair and watched television, accompanied the lady to the bathroom and to work, and sat by her side while she was at work. He would attend every party the lady attended and made a nuisance of himself. When she returned home from work or after a spot of shopping, we knew she was home. We heard him before we saw her. He followed her across the floor, down to the basement, and up again. At crucial meetings with tax accountants and money managers he would cut into their conversation. Like commercials he would stand in the way of enjoyment.

In short, "He" and the old woman are inseparable. It appears a tiny man has taken residence in her throat.

The couple wonders whether they would miss the intruder if he decided to leave as suddenly as he arrived.

The cough, the uncontrollable, persistent, grating cough, right now the cough calls the shots.

56

The Feuding Couple

After five years Peter and Angela's marriage hit a sour note. They had no children. There were constant fights between husband and wife, well known to the neighbors and complete with flying saucers and all.

Angela's mother, who lived just a few blocks away, was regularly kept informed by her daughter of the deteriorating state of the marriage. Angela's mother worried about her daughter because whether through dread or dire distress, Angela began to look like a ghost. Angela believed Peter was having an affair with another woman and was doing his best to get rid of her.

The mother's advice to her daughter was that under no circumstances should she vacate the house. "Don't give in," she counseled.

Peter, finding that Angela was determined to stay on in spite of all the harassment and bullying, decided Angela should be put away.

On a day when Angela was at school teaching he brought a hired killer home; and sitting in the living room, they plotted the murder of Angela.

It was agreed. Peter would go out of state "on business." On a Thursday when Angela worked late, the killer would strangle her as she entered the house. Simple as that. It worked according to plan.

It was customary for Angela's mother to call her daughter after dinner each night. When she called this night, there was no answer.

She called several times, and no one answered the telephone. She walked up to Angela's house, and to her horror she found her daughter dead. Murdered!

She summoned the police, and the husband who was out of town on "business" was notified.

The police inspected for finger prints and took away with them anything that would assist them in their investigation.

A week later the police arrested Peter for the murder of his wife, Angela.

Among the items the police took away with them was the black cylindrical device, Amazon's Alexa, that eavesdrops and records our every conversation.

Alexa in the living room had surreptitiously recorded Peter and the killer plotting Angela's murder.

57

According to plan

The Japs occupied Malaysia during World War II, and Japanese soldiers were given free rein. Malaysians were scared to venture out of their homes. Only those who had jobs and had to provide for their families nervously went out to work and hurried back home early. Schools for the most part were closed. The study of English was forbidden. It was now mandatory that everyone study and speak Japanese. The British currency was withdrawn and Japanese notes of little value were substituted. All street names were changed to Japanese sounding names. The citizens of Malaysia lived in abject fear.

As a rubber producing country, Malaysia's chief export was sneakers manufactured in Kuala Lumpur, the capital of Malaysia. A Japanese army general was appointed in charge of the largest sneaker factory. The general slashed wages and benefits and instituted longer working hours. The factory was put on a war footing.

The general had come to know there was going to be a strike by the workers. He warned the workers that he would throw them all into jail should that happen.

On the day the strike was to take place, soldiers positioned themselves in the factory to ensure there would be no disruption of work. Notices were posted on walls in English, Malay, Chinese and Gujarati warning workers of dire consequences should there be even the slightest disruption of work.

To the surprise of the general when he made a tour of the factory, he observed that everyone turned up for work and worked just as they always did. The general was greatly pleased. He sent a cable to Tokyo that everything was under control. The general received high commendation from the Emperor of Japan, Hirohito.

Two months went by and complaints were pouring in from overseas importers of these sneakers.

The workers, while packing the shoes, placed in each box two rights or two lefts.

58

On my way to Kono

Years ago, many monsoons had come and gone, in another life, in the distant West African state of Sierra Leone while I was employed as accountant in the capital, Freetown, during the harmattan season, I sought to change jobs in mid gallop.

I had an offer for a job as an accountant for a British diamond mining company, Diminco, located in the diamond district of Kono. It was here that the 968.9 carat "Star of Sierra Leone" was discovered, the fourth largest diamond in the world.

It was going to be a rough three-hour ride on dusty terrain. I eased into the window seat of a Greyhound bus with my much traveled leather briefcase and looked out the smeared window.

I saw below me a stout middle-aged, matronly woman, very likely a creole (biracial), in flowered house dress, being kissed passionately, full on the mouth, by a man of great beauty. He was a truly handsome, godlike young guy with blond kinky hair, who was without the least concern for others waiting to board the bus. Their ages by my reckoning suggested that he must be her son. If Adonis had a son, this was he.

Moments later she lumbered into the bus, lurching forward carrying two bulging bags. Most of the seats had now been taken. She commandeered the empty aisle seat next to me as her own. Then, standing tip toe, she pitched one bag into the overhead rack, hurriedly settled into her seat, and leaned toward the window. The beautiful boy was randomly blowing kisses everywhere since he couldn't see where she was because of the dark interior.

"Pardon me," the woman said without so much as a glance at me as she leaned over and tapped the glass. The beautiful boy ran to our window and kissed and kissed, hugging himself with eyes half closed in cosmic ecstasy. Smiling from ear to ear, she kept waving back with matching enthusiasm.

The bus now began to roll.

She slumped into her seat. I turned and faced her squarely. As our eyes locked she said, "Everybody thinks he's my son. But he is not. He's my husband. We've been married five years." She then put her arms tenderly around her bag, and gazing into the distance, she cooed, "We are very happy."

59

Green Card

Aida was walking up and down the living room nervously. She was waiting for her friend Samantha to give her a ride to the Norwalk immigration office for the green card interview. She was headed to the toilet when she heard the knocking sounds of Samantha's sixteen year-old, tumbled down Corolla creaking into the drive way, spewing black smoke from the rear. She forgot all about her mission to the toilet.

"We going to be late. Time up."

"The car wouldn't start. What I can do?"

At the crowded immigration office Aida kept checking into the little mirror from her hand bag, applied rouge to her face, tended to her hair. The doctor has to approve her medical records for her green card.

"Sorry, ma'am, but you can't come in," the nurse said to Samantha.

"I am interpreting," was Samantha's response.

The doctor walked in with the medical records, grimly muttering, "Not good at all."

Facing Samantha, he said, "Ask her if she had TB."

Samantha to Aida: "Doctor wants to know whether you have TV."

Aida to Samantha: "No. Not now. But my ex-husband had. He also had VD."

Doctor to Aida: "In that case we need to test her husband."

Samantha to Aida: "Doctor says he must test your ex-husband's TV and DVD to see whether it works. Otherwise you cannot get your green card. You must know by now everyone in America has TB and VD. Remember! This is not Cuba."

60

The Jumping Jacket

Duke Sudhumatter and his wife, Vanessa, have been taking the Metro North train for over a decade. As was customary with the morning commuters, they would occupy the same seat each day and see the same faces around them. Some in deep slumber, some with their faces buried in the morning newspaper, some feverishly clicking on their computers, and yet others could be seen talking in whispers.

Duke and Vanessa get home each night exhausted from the excruciating demands of their work. They use the one hour twenty minutes of train travel, free from the irritating intrusions of the telephone and television, to discuss, disagree and defer on a wide sweep of topics, from the momentous to the miniscule. Depending on the mood of the moment, the gossip and jocose jabber can in a flash turn into serious colloquy.

Cabined and cribbed within the confinements of the compartment, they had to hear each other out. Where would they finally settle down; when should they retire, what about their son's giddy infatuation for his new girlfriend? "You see, Dookie," Vanessa would say. "All this romance stuff is simply moonshine. When you are courting, as you and I should know, there's a lot of foam and froth, a great deal of fussing and all that, but is she up to it for the long haul? And they would talk about their daughter's penchant for evangelical pursuits. "She's so dependable, Vanes, she has become predictable." Dookie would sweeten the exchange, asking who would be invited for the next Christmas lunch. And so in this fashion they would fill the time, switching back and forth from English to the vernacular with the fluency of a light- fingered pianist running over the black and white keys.

Duke, of frugal construction and dapper in dress, believed if you husband the pennies well, they would beget pounds; and he had a track record to prove it. Vanessa was of the "leave me out of household budgeting" state of mind."

As soon as Duke boarded the train he would remove his jacket, fold it neatly, and place it in the overhead rack. "Why don't you keep the jacket on, Duke, like all the others? I really don't understand" was the daily refrain, and pat would come the response, "I don't want it crushed, I feel warm anyway." With this opening gambit out of the way, Duke Sudhumatter would get cuddly close, nestle by his wife's side and reflect for a few fleeting moments on the menu for their day's discourse.

Duke Sudhumatter was constantly pursued by the haunting fear of being overweight. He would exercise each morning and then, standing in front of the dressing table mirror, look himself over this way and that. At the most inconvenient times of the day or the night he would ask, "Vanes, do you think I have put on weight?"

And Vanessa would come up with the same reply every time. "Duke, why don't you step on the bathroom scale?" and Duke would whimper, "You know how I dread even approaching the machine. That machine can pulverize your personality, crush your ego, and blow it into your eyes in ten seconds. Every time I go for a bath it mocks at me, 'Step on me to see.' The inventor of the personal weighing scale must be hooting and jeering from his grave as Madam Defarge did when witnessing the French aristocrats who were being trundled away in tumbrels to the guillotine. I know when I wear my jacket. Clothes, Vanes, clothes. They are kinder and gentler than those torture machines."

"O.K Duke, do as you wish," Vanes would say. Life proceeded smoothly thus until one day: "Vanes, I have not worn the blazer my son gave me for Christmas for some time. I feel like wearing it." So saying,

Duke Sudhumatter removed the blazer from the closet and, standing foppishly in front of the mirror, tried it on.

"Oh, my god, Vanes, come here immediately. Come quickly," Sudhumatter bellowed. Vanessa, who was toweling after her shower, dropped everything and jumped out to see whether there had been an accident.

"The jacket's tight on me. Can you see? I have put on weight."

"I have told you, Duke, to go slow on those puddings. You will not listen to me."

"I shall have coffee only in the mornings and soup alone for lunch. I shall wear this blazer everyday so I will know when I lose weight."

The couple boarded the train, and Vanessa took her accustomed seat. Duke Sudhumatter went through the motion of placing his jacket on the overhead rack and joined his wife. The pressing topic on the top of the agenda was when each of them should retire. "Before we decide where we are going to settle down, Dookie, we should decide when each of us is going to retire." A spirited discussion ensued.

"Vanes, for well over thirty-five years, even if I may quote Churchill out of context, I have given "my blood, sweat, toil and tears" to my employer. I am plain tired, Vanes. I would like to retire next month and head for home."

"You know, Dookie, you have said this so often it ceases to be a serious proposition." Duke noticed the man who always sat opposite them staring at him. "Vanessa, this chap who is always seated opposite us keeps staring at me." Vanessa looked up by which time the man had turned his gaze away. "Maybe he is gay," she teased. "You will resort to anything, Dookie, to avoid a serious discussion." When they got off the train, Duke noticed the man following him close, almost breathing on his neck. "He's following me." Duke Sudhumatter was agitated.

"You're paranoid, Duke, we're getting late. Let's go." By this time Duke and Vanessa had come up the escalator with the man still behind. At the Grand Central Station entrance the stalker made his way towards Madison Avenue while Duke Sudhumatter and Vanessa went in the direction of First Avenue.

The following day the same man was seated opposite, and he kept glaring at Duke. He followed Duke and Vanessa up the escalator until they parted outside Grand Central Station. Vanessa, too, was now convinced that something was amiss since this went on for a whole week.

Meanwhile Duke Sudhumatter was frenetically working out every morning. He rigidly adhered to his regimen of coffee in the morning, soup alone for lunch. At night he would run down the street, breathing heavily to the accompaniment of barking dogs and the titillation of neighbors. Neighbors peeking through curtains would summon their kids to witness the spectacle of Duke Sudhumatter running around the block. Just as Captain Ahab in Moby Dick was demoniacally driven to capture the white whale that had crippled him, so too Sudhumatter, standing in front of the dressing table mirror, wrestled each morning with the blazer. "I shall overcome," he would hum with a great deal of brio.

The following week Mr. and Mrs. Sudhumatter decided that Duke should flash at this stranger that winsome smile that had caused many a damsel's heart to flutter and swoon, a smile that came easily to him. He should then strike up a conversation. No sooner did Duke take his seat, than he looked at the man and turning on his charm full throttle, with Vanessa observing closely, said, "Hello." He received an icy glare in response.

"It didn't work, Vanes."

"He must be crazy," Vanes cooed.

The couple got off the train, followed by the staring stranger.

Walking towards the information booth inside Grand Central Station, Duke Sudhumatter noticed two policemen giving him the once over.

"I have a feeling the police are watching me closely," said a worried Sudhumatter, and Vanessa agreed.

"Could it be you fit the profile of a terrorist?" Vanessa wondered.

"You see, Vanes, you do not have these problems back home. You will not listen to me about chucking up all this and returning home."

"That's your answer to all our problems," Vanessa countered.

The stalking by the strange passenger and the staring by the policemen went on for three more days until one day . . . .

Duke Sudhumatter and Vanessa were approaching the information booth when Duke felt someone tap his shoulder. Startled, he turned around to find a policeman a foot above him. He had to look up.

"Now the gendarmes are after me," he whispered to his wife. Vanessa was visibly disturbed.

"Sir," the cop began. "Would you mind stepping into my office, please?"

"What is it for?" Sudhumatter demanded.

"Yes, we would like to know," Vanesa joined in

"It's very simple. I'll explain it to you when you come into my office." The three of them trotted into the office. The police officer, sitting on the edge of his desk feigning informality, began.

"I am inspector Dim Dumbell, and you are?"

"My name is Duke Sudhumatter and this is my wife Vanessa." The officer shook hands with both of them.

"Glad to make your acquaintance."

"Could we know why we are here?" Vanessa inquired impatiently.

"Presently, madam, presently. You see we have received a complaint Mr. Soosmatch."

"It is Sudhumatter," Duke corrected, somewhat annoyed.

"That's right," continued the officer. "It has been brought to our notice, Sir, that you are wearing a jacket that does not belong to you. You seem to be both very respectable people. We can settle this amicably without going through a lot of paper work, if you know what I mean. The gentleman standing outside my office has complained that the blazer you are wearing belongs to him."

So saying, Inspector Dumbell stepped out and summoned the man in. It was the staring commuter who customarily sat opposite Sudhumatter.

"So, you maintain this blazer belongs to you?" The officer addressed the question to the newcomer. "Have you any proof?"

The strange passenger who was about the height of Duke with slightly narrower shoulders began speaking.

"My name is Smelly Wrongshoe. I live in Bridgeport and my office is on Madison Avenue. I am not accusing the gentleman of stealing. I'm certain it's a genuine mistake. Inadvertently he may have taken my jacket. Now if you will observe officer, the jacket is ill-fitting on him."

(Duke recalled – I always felt uncomfortable in this)

"I have my business card tucked away in the breast pocket. It may be there still."

At the officer's request Duke Sudhumatter removed the jacket and handed it over to him. The officer ran his fingers through the pockets and pulled out a business card. It read: Smelly Wrongshoe. Environmentalist. It had a Madison Avenue office address and Washington Avenue home address.

"Let me see you wear this." The officer then passed the jacket over to Smelly. Smelly slipped it over his frame effortlessly as he would his foot into an old shoe.

"You see, Mr. Shoematter," the officer began and Duke corrected "Sudhumatter."

"That's right (now with a broad smile), if the jacket does not fit, I cannot acquit. What do you wish to do, Mr. Shoemaker?"

"Mr. Sudhumatter, if you don't mind."

"That's right. What do you wish to do, sir?"

Sudhumatter now looked at Vanessa and replied with visible relief. "If it does not fit, I quit. He can keep it. Well, all I can say is it very closely resembles the one I had." Then turning around to Smelly he asked, "Why could you not have approached me and verified without this circus?'

"I have been trying to do so for a long time. I tried to catch you alone so as not to embarrass your wife but the two of you are inseparable. Are you newly married? You both are like Romeo and Cleopatra."

Vanessa had by now reached the bitter extremity of her patience. With effort she suppressed the volcanic fury that was rising within her. She straightened herself to her full height. She looked into the eyes of Wrongshoe. She transfixed him with her laser like glare. Vanessa's tone now turned combative. She shot back with the self-assurance of a savant with particular emphasis on the name "SMELLY." She enunciated, "You mean Romeo and Juliet and Anthony and Cleopatra.

For an ominous thirty seconds, no one spoke. The reader will be eager to know how each one would have appeared to a passer-by.

Inspector Dim Dumbell had the air of one who had cracked open a baffling case like a coconut. Smelly Wrongshoe turned his gaze away from the rest in embarrassment, holding tightly to the jacket like a little lad who had got back his toy. Vanessa was getting late for an important meeting she was presiding over that morning. The contours of her face contorted, she was like the Olympics one-hundred meter sprinter, restless at the starting block, ready to go at the crack of the pistol.

What was happening to the protagonist, Sudhumatter? A beatific smile descended upon him and in slow motion the smile leisurely crawled across his face as would a toddler across the floor. A feeling of unfettered joy filled his heart, his soul, and every bone in his body. He was glowing like an incandescent tube of light in a dark room. He was jubilant. Calmness settled over Duke Sudhumatter. And he was now breathing easily. Dookie turned around to his Cleopatra, to his Juliet, to his Vanes and trilled like a bird in spring time: "Darling, this means I have not put on weight."

Inspector Dim Dumbell broke the conversational log jam.

"Well, gentlemen." he pompously announced. "Shall we wrap this up with a handshake?"

Duke and Smelly shook hands, exchanged business cards and departed. While leaving, Duke heard Smelly whisper to officer Dumbell, "See you at Aunty Matilda's tonight."

The day was nippy and Duke Sudhumatter was sans blazer. During the lunch hour he walked up to Macy's and bought a smart jacket on sale.

A week went by. It was a Saturday morning, and Sudhumatter was walking towards his garage. He was going to take Vanessa to Kennedy airport when he saw the mailman bring a parcel. He opened it and to his consternation saw an old jacket, one like his. He tried it on. It went around him snugly like Caesar's toga. Then it struck him. "Let me try his pockets." Inside the inner breast pocket there was a business card. It read: "Smelly Wrongshoe. Environmentalist"

"Jumping Jacket, Vanessa, come and see this" he yelled out.

61

Twin Path – A Ten Dollars Worth

N ada had twins, Para and Sara. On their twenty-first birthday Nada took them both to the river that runs along their home and on the bank of the river said to them, "Here's one thousand dollars for each of you. I do not wish to see either of you for the next ten years. On your thirty-first birth day we will meet here. I'd like to see what you both have made of yourselves.

Para got a job as a filing clerk in a law firm, worked nights as a watchman at the law library; he worked long and hard, days and nights and on weekends and eventually passed out as a lawyer and a good one at that, making lots of money.

Sara made his way to the Himalayas, and there at the feet of a holy swami learnt all the mantras and practiced long hours of meditation under his tutelage.

On the appointed day, their thirty-first birthday, Nada, Para and Sara met on the banks of the river.

Father Nada asked Para and Sara, "What have you to show me for the ten years you have been away?

Sara with a broad confident smile walked on water and got across to the other side. Para summoned the boat man standing nearby and, giving ten dollars said, "Here, take my dad and me over to the other side."

62

Cripples in demand

In this West African country where I lived and worked for many years, children born with deformities, crippled, withered, blind, lame are in great demand. The more grotesque the deformity, the greater was the demand. Competing enterprises have agents in hospitals who will promptly inform them as soon as a child with deformity is born. Heads of these businesses swoop upon the miserable parents of these children and bid for them.

The successful businessman, now the owner of these cripples, houses them in a building away from public view and feeds and clothes them.

In the wee hours of the morning before day break, these cripples are transported in a van and are dropped off at public places like busy bus stands and train stations. Members of the public moved by the sight of these pathetic kids throw coins at them.

At the end of the day a supervisor will arrive in a van and pick up the cripples and the money and take them to their lodging. It's big business.

This whole process is repeated the following day, every day.

63

Break the rules

You always follow the rules. Can't you once do something crazy? Give voice to your wild side, if you have one. You worship routine. Day after day it's the same. To the gym in the morning Monday thru Thursday, cooking thereafter, dinner at six, with your parents on the telephone thereafter, then it's time for bed. It's the same the next day and the day thereafter for week after week. Could we not travel a little and see the world? There is so much to see: Monet and Rembrandt, Rodin's "Thinker" and Michelangelo's "David", the Taj Mahal, the Pyramids, the Eiffel Tower. O God, there is so much to see and experience and so little time left. So saying, Anton left her for good, never to return.

Angela went to her bed room and ruminated. Yes, Anton is right. I should do something wild. It feels good just thinking about it. So here I am, ready to break the rules.

From now on I will go to the gym from Tuesday thru Friday, not Monday thru Thursday.

64

In search of "The Average American"

J ust as H. M. Stanley went in search of the Scottish missionary and
explorer Dr. Livingston in Central Africa, I am in search of the
"Average American" here in the United States of America.

If you find him, would you please contact me?

You will recall the Republican nominee for president of the United
States of America, Senator John McCain, is reported to have stated, "I mean,
the fact is [Ahmadinejad's] the acknowledged leader of that country and you
may disagree, but that's, uh, that's your right to do so, but I think if you
asked any *Average American* who the leader of Iran is, I think they'd know."

Can any one by looking at a person say he or she is or is not the
"Average American" to whom Mr. McCain is referring?

Is there a yardstick by which to measure or a litmus test we can
apply to identify an "Average American"? Haven't we heard a teacher
replying, "He's average," to the question, "How is Tom doing in class?"
The teacher means Tom is neither too bright nor totally dumb, certainly
not the sharpest tool in the shed.

When they say "Average American," is this average arrived at on an
income high and low or on academic achievements?

If income, which is the high point and which the low? If based on
scholastic achievements, what is the threshold?

I doubt when Mr. McCain is referring to "Average Americans," he had
in mind patricians like Bush, Baker, and Kennedy. Generally, when we

say average, we mean "ordinary," and I doubt we can label the Kennedys, the Bushes and the Baker Brahmins all "ordinary." By ordinary I mean just another face in the crowd, sometimes referred to as a statistic.

Why do we not consider them ordinary? Is it because you have a fixed mental picture of them as being affluent and of having graduated from the leading colleges in the country? Is it something to do with the color of their blood being blue, the so called blue-blooded aristocracy in addition to the color of their skin?

High school graduates, plumbers, carpenters, the non- college educated, white, blue collar, lunch pail working class on shift sometimes referred to as "invisible Americans" - are they the "Average Americans"?

What about women in comfortable financial circumstances who never saw the inside of a university, have no need to earn a living, who burn daylight gamboling and gossiping with friends at country clubs? Are they the "Average Americans"?

Those homeless in shelters! They do not count? If there is an "Average American," by the same token could there be an above "Average American" and a below "Average American"? If so, who are they?

Is the "Average American" in New England different from the "Average American," say, in Georgia or Mississippi? If so, in what way, may I ask? Are there common traits like a kind of lowest common denominator?

Is not every human being special, endowed with some unique quality that the next person does not possess? To call someone "average" in this context, is it not tantamount to condescension? Does it not give the impression, when someone refers to a section of the people as "average," he is placing himself socially a cut above those he is referring to as "average"?

Or is the notion of "Average American" a mutable concept, a vague reference to general consensus, a substitute for "in the opinion of a majority of Americans"?

Is this the profile of the "Average American"?

- He (for this purpose he includes she) would live within spitting distance of Dunkin Donuts, Wal Mart, C.V.S. Pharmacy, Stop and Shop and the bank.

- You will not find him shopping at Nieman Marcus or Bloomingdales. Perhaps, Sears, Target and J.C. Penny.
- He would at the supermarket check-out counter pull out fistful of coupons and scrutinize them. Some not applicable, some expired, and he would finally tender the appropriate ones, while all this time holding up a line of ten or more.
- He would keep a close watch of the cash monitor to ensure that the proper price is being charged.
- He would not buy anything that is not on sale - "Two for the price of one" being his favorite.
- In a city he would go in circles looking for a parking spot on the side road for his car rather than pay at a garage.
- His reading is mainly limited to the local newspapers and the television news he gets is from CNN in snippets while changing clothes.
- At a restaurant after a meal he would indicate to the waiter that he would like the left-over "doggy bagged."
- His "Trinity" is Football, Baseball and Basketball. He takes to the bleachers, beer and popcorn in hand, like a duck to water. In these surroundings he feels free and liberated like a mosquito in a nudist colony.
- In the mornings on his way to work he will grab a cup of coffee at his favorite deli and drive away in his pick-up, sipping the coffee and steering the vehicle simultaneously, while listening to Limbaugh or Imus.
- He spends his vacation not in travel but working around the house, completing his basement or renovating the kitchen. These projects are hardly ever finished, much to the annoyance of his wife.
- He and his spouse may be working two jobs, working overtime, just in order to provide for their children basic amenities and a better life than they have had.
- You can see him lining up at the local "Seven Eleven" for his weekly Lotto ticket.

- He will park the car in the driveway and pack his garage with tools, the lawn mower, and all else in between.
- He will borrow a book from the library rather than buy online.
- In him there is a sense of fair play.
- He will donate generously and willingly to ameliorate the hardships of total strangers, as was seen for instance after the devastation caused by a tsunami in Southeast Asia.
- He loves the U.S.A. and is grateful for the opportunities it has afforded him and his children.
- He is quick to smile and slow to anger.
- He feels there is nowhere else in the world where he can rise to great heights in any discipline if he works hard enough.
- He never forgets that this is a land of immigrants from every corner of the globe and a country ruled by laws to which everyone must submit.
- He will willingly join in community work for the general good.
- He is fully aware that his country is not perfect, that there are many problems of social and economic inequities, but he takes pride in the fact that his country is the best one going in the world today.
- In times of crisis he is united, putting aside ethnic, religious, and political prejudices as was seen in the aftermath of the 9/11 terrorist attack.

65

The Lovers

Seated in the open veranda of my parents' home in Chankanai in arid Jaffna province, in the north of Ceylon, from where I could see the post office within walking distance of the only bicycle repair shop, the fish market, church, a temple, the zinc - roofed cinema hall where shows are cancelled when it rains--far, far from the madding crowd of Colombo, I see boys walking jauntily in a pack after school, following girls on their way home. The boys have books in one hand, strapped by a cord, and with the other they are gesticulating in boisterous banter. I could hear them: "Nice frock she is wearing," one would say. "She's the girl for you," another would comment.

Sathyavan, "Sathya" as he was called, would sing aloud love songs from recent movies, directing them to Savithri to the chuckles of her friends. This is how Sathya made his rambling overtures to Savithri each day, leisurely ambling behind her up to her house. Savithri, walking amidst the giggling gaggle of girls and flashing her flirtatious smile, encouraged Sathya.

"Sathya likes you, Sav. That song is meant for you," her friends would tease her; and Savi would protest, "No men, he is just being naughty." Savithri welcomed the attention, and she too liked Sathya.

Ponnammah observed all this through the holes in her cadjan fence partition. She did not like what she witnessed; she had a foreboding of impending calamity--a scandal that was sure to spin out of control, she reckoned. She was convinced Savithri's parents should be forewarned.

How could she do it? Being of lower caste, "Pariah" to be precise, she had scant access to Savithri's home. And yet the mother in her urged her on. So, she mentioned it to the toddy tapper, the toddy tapper made it known to the dhoby, and the dhoby passed it on to the barber who shaved and barbered Savithri's father in the open yard of his home. This is how neighborhood watch worked in these parts.

"What is this, Savi? I hear you are flirting with boys while returning home from school," her father inquired in a minatory tone.

"No, Appah, I come only with girls," she replied obliquely. "No, I cannot have this. Even a whiff, the slightest smell of gossip, however unfounded, will ruin your chances of marriage. Your brother Karnan will in future come to fetch you," her father decreed.

Female chastity was the bedrock of this culture's code of honor. Girls were required to guard chastity like Silas Marner, his gold, like a brood of hen her eggs. And therefore Karnan, twelve years-old, would go every day to his sister's school and escort her home along with her friends. This posed a problem to Sathya. The fiends conferred. Kullan, the shrewd one, said: "I know Karnan loves Superman comics. I will win him over with a steady supply, and you will be in good shape, my friend."

It worked. Sathya continued to walk with his friends behind Savi but avoided making amorous comments. Karnan became the messenger, carrying letters between the starry-eyed lovers. The purity, intensity, innocence, and the pain of passion in their yearning hearts were all poured into these scented missives.

Karnan would inform Sathya which temple festival Savi would attend, and Sathya with his friends was there. Temple festivals are a big deal in these parts. Mothers powdered, painted, jeweled, and splendidly upholstered their marriageable daughters and paraded them for all to see.

If their eyes met just once, Savi and Sathya would go home thrilled to the soles of their feet. In public places mothers and aunts, with their prying eyes, kept unmarried girls on a short leash. Their eyes like the beams of a lighthouse would sweep without ceasing through the hall, looking out for recalcitrant urchins with errant motives. They were grounded in the dictum that "a closely watched pot does not boil over."

Sathya passed the university entrance examination and went to Colombo, while Savi on completing the General Certificate Ordinary Level was removed from school. Sathya wrote once a week to Savi. The letters were sent to Kullan who was now working in an automobile repair shop, and he would pass them on to Savi's brother for Savi.

Sathya would spell out all that took place almost by the hour--his science lectures, his new friends, not one incident was missed. Savi would likewise account for her movements, which were for the most part uneventful. Although to date not a spoken word passed between them, so graphic and detailed were they in their correspondence that the absence of face-to-face meetings in no way diminished their ardor. They were so frank in their outpourings they even planned their lives together as husband and wife.

Sathya had now passed the final examination and was a graduate in science with a temporary teaching job in a nearby school. It was time to talk marriage, the lovers agreed.

"How do I set about it?" Sathya inquired of his street-smart friend Kullan.

"Look here Sathya," Kullan counseled. "Under no circumstances should this affair appear to be a love match. That's a no- no. The whole thing will blow up. Savi's and Karnan's bones will be broken. We must make it look like a proposed marriage. I know a marriage broker. I will grease his palm and he will do the rest."

It was agreed.

And so, one fine day in the midst of the Hindu Deepavali festivities the broker, his palms now well- greased, went over to Savi's house with the marriage proposal.

"Yes, I would like to have my daughter married. Tell me more about the young man," Savi's father demanded with feigned casualness.

"He's a fine boy, sir. Does not drink or smoke. A regular temple goer, he is not greedy for a big dowry. All he wants is a good, modest, well brought-up girl. I think your daughter fits the description. He has friends in Africa who are trying to get a job for him there. They are paid very well there, you know." The broker then proceeded to fill the father

in with details of the family background, placing emphasis on being of
Vellala caste.

"I need time to think about it. Come back next week," her father replied.

The father, now very excited and taking two steps at a time, dashed
to his wife in the kitchen saying, "Kunjoo, there's a proposal for Savi.
Fine boy! Good caste. He is sure to get a job in Africa. Does not smoke
or drink. Not interested in big dowry. This is luck by chance, Kunjoo."

The wife, always to the point, inquired, "What did you say to the broker?"

"I did not want to show I was thrilled. I said I needed time to think
about it; now, not a word to your sister. Next thing the whole village will
be talking about it. Go and discreetly check on the family and caste of
this boy. If everything is okay, we can quickly have the registration and
the wedding after a year when we have saved enough money."

The mother made the usual checks and found them to be satisfactory.
The parents of Savi and Sathya exchanged courtesy visits, and in a
few weeks a Notary Public witnessed the signing of documents which
conferred on the couple the legal status of man and wife.

"Savi," said her father, "Sathya can come here to visit you. But until
the wedding is over you cannot go out with him. We do not allow girls
to go out until they are properly married, do you understand?"

Savi, looking at her toes, nodded ascent.

Sathya, who was five-foot eight, wishbone slim, of fair complexion,
wavy hair and sparkling eyes, would come daily immediately after school,
sit in the front veranda, and talk to Savi. Savi, who was willowy and well
groomed, pranced all day like a young calf, humming her favorite tunes
from the latest hits (whistling by girls is taboo) and would have dolled
up for Sathya's visit.

Savi's mother would be seated all the while in the living room,
ostensibly reading the newspaper, "Thinakaran," out of sight but within
earshot. Sathya and Savi continued to communicate their love through
letters. This was the only vehicle by which they gave expression to their
smoldering passion.

When Sathya went home one day after a visit to Savi, there was a
telegram from the principal of Waterloo School for Boys and Girls in

Sierra Leone offering a teaching job. If interested, he should proceed immediately, it stated. On Sathya's last visit to Savi, as he was about to leave, her father said, "Savi, you could go up to the gate and wish Sathya "Good-bye." At the gate Sathya held Savi's hand and whispered, "I shall return in one year when your parents will be ready for the wedding, we'll get married, and we both can return to Sierra Leone. Until then we will each write a letter a week giving all the news."

Savi and her parents began making feverish preparations for the wedding. Savi and her mother, accompanied by an aunt, went to India and purchased the koorai sari and other accoutrements. Relatives and friends of like caste jumped into the frenzy of preparations for the wedding with gusto. Arrangements were made to collect carpets, cooking utensils, lamps and lanterns for the wedding. Work on the pandal to accommodate the guests was to begin soon on an auspicious day determined by the temple priest. Velan, the expert in this kind of work, was informed. Relatives and neighbors, hearing the glad tidings, visited at all hours to express their joy. Savithri would rush from kitchen to guests, gamboling in their company, serving coffee or uncooled Orange Barley soda purchased from the boutique. Her friends teased her and playfully taunted her. Savithri, with the coyness becoming a bride, lapped it all up in good humor for she was convinced she was on the cusp of a new life of passion and connubial ecstasy.

In Sierra Leone Sathya was met at the airport by his friend Skanda, who had arranged the job, and the school's principal. A two- bedroom college flat was allocated to him. Like his compatriot teachers, he bought a four-year old Volkswagen car on a loan from Barclays Bank. He would remain indoors, prepare his school work, and write to Savi about Sierra Leone, the school, the habits and customs of the natives, his car, and his friends.

A few months went by. One Sunday Skanda along with the other Ceylonese teachers visited Sathya and said to him, "Look here, Sathya, you cannot remain indoors all the time. Weekends are for fun. Be a weekend warrior. We visit Tejan's bar and have a few beers. C'mon, join us."

Reluctantly Sathya went along. Khadijah, the daughter of Tejan, the owner, was always at the service counter. An attractive, ebullient girl, full of verve, bubbling with buoyant effervescence, she was the cynosure of all who frequented the bar. Khadijah was constantly surrounded by noisy, belligerent boys and was tired of them. She saw in Sathya a shy, respectful, good-looking "Indian boy." Sathya found Khadijah's loose and easy ways attractive. He admired the way she handled the tipsy patrons, bouncing from one customer to the next, pandering to their needs.

Sathya began frequenting the bar alone. Waterloo, a tiny village approximately fifty miles from the capital, had very little to offer by way of entertainment. Transported across thousands of miles from south Asia and transplanted to an alien land in West Africa, the loneliness Sathya experienced was lacerating. In Khadijah he found an accommodating companion with whom he could communicate free of native inhibitions. He would wait until the bar closed and then accompany her to her house nearby.

Khadijah's father, noticing this increasing familiarity between them, said to Khadijah, "Why do you dismiss your friend at the gate? He could come and have meals with us. Let me tell you this, Khadi, if you think he will marry you, forget about it. Indians marry only Indians."

"Pa," Khadijah replied reverentially, "I think Satty is different from others."

"Look here, daughter, the only difference between two Indians is the name and that too seldom."

Meanwhile Sathya's letter writing became sporadic and sparse in content. Savithri's letters were lying around the flat unopened. Savi grew depressed. Savi's father communicated this to Sathyavan's father, Thasan. Thasan wrote a letter to the principal of Waterloo School for Boys and Girls inquiring about his son's health, informing him of his concern over his silence.

The principal, aware of what was going on, paid no heed to the letter. Savi's depression grew worse. Sathya's mother on her visit to see her daughter-in-law was moved by her condition. She went home and said to her husband, "Send a telegram to Sathya that I am very ill. Doctors do not give me much time."

Mothers know intuitively that this special arrow in their quiver never misses the mark. The umbilical attachment between mother and child is never severed.

Sathya on receiving the telegram got special permission to travel and arrived at the Palali airport in the north of Ceylon. In a matter of days he was married to Savi. Two days after the wedding the couple departed for Sierra Leone. Sathya had to pay for his wife's airfare.

On the day Savithri arrived at the flat Sathya, pointing to the larger of the two rooms, said, "Henceforth that will be your room and I will be occupying the other room."

"Why do we have to sleep in separate rooms?" Savi wanted to know.

"I work till very late and my hours are irregular. That's why," he replied.

From the time they arrived at their flat in Sierra Leone Sathya had nothing to do with his wife. Savithri never left the flat. He forbade his friends visiting his home. "She's not quite right, machan," he would say touching his head with his index finger. Sathya continued to spend all his nocturnal hours with Khadijah, coming home only to sleep and that too seldom. Savithri could not communicate with her parents. She did not have the money, the means, or the wherewithal to mail her letters. Letters from her parents were addressed to Sathya's school and he destroyed them.

Growing up like a nun in a cloistered home, Savithri was now condemned to loneliness and neglect within the confines of the flat, living her life only in romantic imagination. As dream-like days turned into nights and sleepless nights changed to dawn conjoined by misery, her mind was afflicted. Unglued from its moorings, her mind was adrift like a cork on the ocean. Her unkempt appearance, her ungroomed hair now like a floor mop, the faraway look in her eyes glazed and unshining, all confirmed a mind adrift. Like Ophelia in Hamlet she began to ramble and sing snatches of songs. When Sathya left for school, Savithri, still in her night clothes that hung on her unevenly, would sit mute at the entrance to the building or shamble in the yard laughing without reason.

This soon became an embarrassment to the other Ceylonese teachers in the school. So one day Sathya's friend Skanda and two other Ceylonese teachers took Sathya to a bar far away from Tejan's and implored that he should make up with Savi and that it was time he broke up with Khadijah.

Sathya, raising his voice, blurted out, "I was tricked into this marriage. I do not want to have anything to do with her." So saying, he confirmed his giddy infatuation for Khadijah and his visceral indifference towards Savithri.

"Yes, I love Khadi. You are wasting your time." Sathya was inflexible.

"In that case send her back, Sathya. This is an embarrassment to all of us. Can't you see her mind is affected?" Skanda pleaded.

"She was already crazy when I married her, Skanda. I do not mind her being sent back, but I have no money for her passage. I'm already in debt from paying for her passage here."

"This has become the talk of the town, Sathya. What we will do is this: we will send the hat round and collect enough money for her passage. You pay us back when you are able to do so," Skanda proposed.

This was agreed. A collection was initiated. Tejan made a significant contribution. Sathya and Skanda took Savithri to the Lungi airport and with the assistance of a flight assistant saw her boarded on British Caledonian Airways.

Sathya never returned to Ceylon. Like retreating soldiers, he cut the wires and destroyed the bridges behind him. Like a slithering snake that sheds its skin, Sathyavan shuffled off to begin a new life. He now lives with Khadijah and their children.

And what became of Savithri?

She, who was made to sacrifice at the altar of social conformity and conventional morality the tactile happiness of the moment, who was made to exchange the palpable pleasure of the present for society's promise of future rewards, was left holding an empty and meaningless promise.

In the deep, dark, pitiful cavern of her tormented mind she began to hear voices and the decibel of discordant notes. In her mind the clanging and banging grew louder and louder. Minutes appeared to her like hours and hours a never-ending day. Her heart could no longer carry the weight of sadness, of disappointment in a dream that never even once saw the light of day.

And so, dear reader, on a day when her parents were away attending a wedding, driven by a deranged mind and a heart impaled, torn and rent asunder by grief, deprived of the soaring joys of the flesh, Savithri took her life by swallowing a potion of the local arsenic, Polidol.

The parents of Savithri and the friends of Savithri's parents wonder, sadly: is murder committed only by wielding a weapon?

Thus ended, star-crossed, the love and life of a once starry-eyed lover still in full bloom.

As the poet Thomas Gray in his elegy so eminently and with prescience tells us:

"Full many a flower of purest serene,
The dark unfathomed caves of ocean bear,
Full many a flower is born to blush unseen,
And waste its sweetness in the desert air."

Ceylon – Now called Sri Lanka

Colombo – Capital of Sri Lanka

Toddy – An inebriating drink extracted from coconut

Tapper – The man who climbs the coconut tree to secure the toddy

Dhoby - The man who visits homes, collects soiled clothes, washes them, and brings them back--for a fee of course.

Appah - Dad

Vellala – Farmer caste

Machan – Bro or Buddy

66

The Jaffna Man

The tiny island of Sri Lanka in the Indian Ocean, which used to be called Ceylon and is about the size of West Virginia, had during my time there in the sixties a population of about eleven million. Of that population three million are Tamils who are culturally, linguistically, and by religious persuasion markedly different from the majority community, the Sinhalese.

The Tamils occupied the peninsula, which came to be known as Jaffna, on the northern tip of the island, hanging on by a toe, cheek by jowl, to South India with whom they had close cordial cultural bonds. The Tamils of Ceylon being a minority like the Coptic Christians in Egypt, the Rohingya Muslims of Myanmar, the Shias in Saudi Arabia, the Sunnis in Iran, and like people of color in the United States--in fact, like all minorities everywhere--suffered from feelings of insecurity.

The insecurity they felt was further amplified for the Jaffna Man by the fact that Jaffna was arid, hot, and humid, the last place you want to engage in farming. The Jaffna Man mostly owned a postage stamp size land, which was dowered daughter down. On this tiny plot of land he cultivated rice and some vegetables for his daily diet. I recall my grand parents' postage stamp of a plot.

By sheer force of compelling circumstances, the Jaffna Man became self-reliant and industrious, embracing education as his first and last refuge. Every father wanted his son to become a doctor and his daughter to marry one, failing which the son should enter government service wherein he saw security and a steady income. Most Jaffna men at this time were employed in government service in the capital, Colombo, and lived together with other Jaffna men in cramped spaces in small, low rent apartments (called "chummeries"), cutting corners with their chums chummily. They were mostly single, having left wife and kids back home, and they would dash off during long weekends to be with the family.

Kandiah Murugesu, fondly called by friends "Murugs," was very blessed. He had the ideal job. He worked for the government in Jaffna town, seven miles away from his village. Every day he would leave home at eight in the morning, take the bus, and return home by five in the evening. The weekends were all his to attend weddings, funerals and take care of his ailing, aging mother.

One day Murugs received a telegram from the government in Colombo which read:

YOU ARE HEREBY INFORMED YOU HAVE BEEN TRANSFERRED TO COLOMBO. THE TRANSFER WILL TAKE EFFECT TWO WEEKS FROM DATE OF THIS LETTER.

Murugs went dizzy. He was shattered. His heart beat like a hammer inside him. He translated the contents to his wife. By this time the entire village knew about it. The Post Master had informed the messenger, and the messenger told everyone. Each village is different from the next. Chankanai, my mother's birthplace, is different from Sandilipay, that of my father. How news travels in a village is a mystery not easily understood. Women spread it over fences, standing on tip-toe. In a flash the nerves of the village were pulsating with the news.

Murugs had to do something soon to cancel this order. He must go to Colombo immediately and meet with influential Tamils, colloquially referred to as "Namadayal," to enlist their support. (Namadayal are the Tamil equivalent of the Italian "Amica Nostra.") But first he had to find a place to stay one night.

According to Tamil custom your father's brother's children and your mother's sister's children are referred to as "cousin brother" and "cousin sister." Murugs had an older cousin brother living in Wellawatte in Colombo. The cousin brother wrote back to say he would be glad to accommodate him.

Murugs left his village of Chankanai by bus at six in the evening with a dinner parcel prepared by his wife Pon, and he boarded the train "Yarl Devi" at eight in the evening. Being of frugal disposition, a character trait of the Jaffna Man, he bought a third-class ticket, facetiously called "Gandhi Class," spent a sleepless journey to Colombo, arrived at the Fort station at six in the morning, took the bus to his cousin brother's, left his change of clothes in the cousin brother's house, set out immediately to the head government office, and went from one office to the next. Finally, around eight o'clock at night he was able to have the transfer order rescinded. He had not had a morsel of food or a sip of water all day. Famished beyond words, he set out for his cousin brother's house.

At cousin brother's house the brother and his wife were seated on the balcony waiting for Murugs. They ordinarily have dinner at six thirty. They waited until eight o'clock and still Murugs had not come. Assuming Murugs would by now have had his dinner at Ananda Bhavan, a popular eating house near the government offices, they sat down to have their meal. Around nine o'clock they finished their dinner; and after clearing the dishes and cleaning up the kitchen, they resumed their chit-chat on the balcony.

It was around ten o'clock when Murugs turned up. The brother said on seeing him "Look here, Thamby (younger brother), you must be very tired, your room is all made up, you go to bed we will talk in the morning."

Murugs had no choice. Saying "Om Annah" (yes, brother), he changed and got into bed. Thinking he would give his brother a hint, he came out of his room saying, "Annah, did you call, me?" "No, Thamby (younger brother), go to bed; we'll talk in the morning." Murugs tried once more with the same result. Giving it up as a lost cause, he went to bed very hungry.

Murugs had to catch the eight o'clock "Yarl Devi" to Jaffna the following day. He woke up very early in the morning and without making any noise lest he wake "Annah" and "Anni" (cousin brother and sister-in-law) left for the bus station. The very thought that he could remain in his village brought the color back to his cheeks, old time gaiety to his eye, and put the joy of life back in his heart.

Veni vidi vici" – I came – I saw - I conquered. Mission Accomplished, he beamed.

67

The Long-Held Secret

In the evenings during the summer my wife and I go for walks along Whitney Avenue, the capstone to a peaceful day--and we are grateful for it.

I see men and women--sometimes single, arms swinging; sometimes in pairs holding hands; some walking briskly, some leisurely; the athletic jogging solo or with a baby stroller in tow; all walking in the opposite direction.

Should we see someone puttering about in their front garden, we exchange pleasantries and then move on.

The next summer we are happy to see them; and they us, I would think. Should I not see any of the regulars, my mind begins to wander. Has he passed on? Been transferred to another state? It cannot be! He did not appear to be in active employment. Kind of in tranquil retirement, I believed.

And yet who knows? Perhaps he is too ill to be jogging or briskly walking along Whitney Avenue and is confined to bed. Perhaps the children who live out of state have come and taken him away to be with them since he can no longer take care of his needs. This is what must have happened to Paddy who, standing on dignity and cherishing his independence, stubbornly refused to live with his well-off children out of state even though severely incapacitated. We patronize the same library. Across the aisle I could see him scanning the obituary notices, and I would call out to him, "If ever you see my name there, you should give me a call." And he would answer, "No, I don't see your name." I don't see him anymore. Perhaps he is somewhere in a Senior Home. Who can tell me?

I live in a condominium complex in the shadow of a senior home. At all hours of the day and night I see ambulances and fire engines shrilly taking residents away. Is it to the ICU? Is it to the morgue? I do not wish to know. I cannot be of any help. I pray they have a peaceful passage "Home."

I used to work in New York City. The office where I worked was within sneezing distance of Grand Central Station. Lunch time during the summer I would walk across to the station to see the many fun things that go on there, especially around the information booth. The "Information Booth"- this is the meeting place of men, women and children descending upon the city from cities everywhere. Choirs singing, curios on sale, acrobats displaying their talent, guitarist strumming away, first time visitors gazing up at the multi-colored dazzling dome-shaped ceiling preserved for posterity by Jackie Kennedy, slow-moving lines for fast food, commuters too early for the train idling and then those with minutes to spare hurrying down the steps to catch the train about to whistle away . . . and there's much more.

Here in Grand Central Station you can hear and feel the heartbeat of New York City.

On onr fine sunny day, I began walking from Vanderbilt Avenue towards the section of Grand Central Station where taxis line up, thinking of my friends living in various countries whom I had not seen in a long time. I was in jacket, coat and tie, starched shirt and pressed pants since that's what the kind of work I did demanded of me. From a distance I see a male, one legged, a crutch under his right arm holding out a tin cup in his left. I had not seen him before. My heart went out to him.

How much can he collect this way? Would it be enough for even half of one meal? Where on earth does he sleep? By this time, I had come up to him. And he says, looking straight into my eyes, in crisp, clear accent:

"Life is not all that bad. Cheer up."

What he meant was, "Mister! You look pathetic. You put me off."

68

The Medical Merry Go-Round

D ick was handing me a book I had requested from the library. I
noticed on his left index finger there was a swelling and I asked:
"What's that swelling, Dick?"

He replied: "I have no idea, Chandra, it's been there many years."

"Does it hurt?"

"No, not really. At times there's a slight tingle, that's about it."

"Is it getting bigger?"

"Over a period of years, yes, I would say."

"I think you should have it checked out."

A couple of months later I saw Dick again. Stone the crows!, there
was no swelling.

"Dick! I don't see that swelling. Whatever happened?"

"It's a long story, Chandra."

"Tell me all about it."

"My daughter-in-law, who understands these things, insisted I see
a doctor. I call a Primary Care Physician of her recommendation. The
lady at the doctor's office asks:

"Have you been here before?"

"No."

"Do you have insurance?"

"Yes, the Zig Zag Insurance of America."

"The doctor can see you next week Wednesday at 2 P.M. There will be a co-payment of $40.00, which must be paid in advance. If you do not turn up without giving twenty-four hours notice, there's a penalty."

Dick continues: "At the appointed time I turned up at the doctor's office. I was weighed and measured and taken to another room. The doctor checked my pulse. Looked into my eyes. Peeled back one eye lid, then the other. And then inserted something into my ears. Listened to My heart and lungs with his stethoscope. He pressed his fingers here and there on my abdomen and finally examined the 'sick' finger."

Doctor:" You have to see a dermatologist."

"They had not finished taking an inventory of my body parts. He then instructed his assistant to make the appointment. I was told I could see the specialist the following Friday at three o'clock.

On Wednesday I received a call from the doctor's office and went over the same routine as earlier about copay, et cetera.

As scheduled I appeared at the specialist's office, and after the payment formalities were concluded I was ushered into the doctor's office.

The doctor very closely examined the finger with due care and caution and pronounced that it calls for surgery. He then turned to his assistant and said she should make the appointment for me.

On hearing this my head began to spin, thinking what all this is going to cost. So, I said to the doctor, 'Does not seem serious, doctor. I'll come another day.'"

"What did the doctor say?" I ask.

"Sometimes these swellings have a curious effect. There will be apparent improvement, and then – poof. You are in big trouble.

I felt rage and distrust melting toward fear. You see, Chandra, what do I know about these things? Perhaps this doctor does. How can I take a chance of pitting my ignorance against the doctor's professional knowledge and years of experience? I felt trapped, Chandra, like so many before me and as certainly so many after me.

The appointment was made for surgery for Friday two weeks hence.

On Monday of the week of the surgery I got a call and was informed that I should:

A. Have a physical done.
B. Have a chest ex-ray done.

I went through all these, coughing up a copay every time.

On the day prior to the day of the surgery the surgeon's office called and advised me as follows.

A. I should have someone drive me to and from surgery.
B. I should come in comfortable clothes.

On the day of the surgery my daughter in law drove me to the place where surgery was to be performed. On the way she noticed the "sick" finger was messy. She pulled over to the shoulder, and we both examined the finger. The boil had burst (pfft!) and pus was oozing out.

At the surgeon's office the doctor says to me, "You lucky man. Nature has come to your assistance." The assistant cleaned the finger with antiseptic and sent me home."

Chandra! I was worried. I am a temp and every time I took leave I was not paid.

After Evelyn left me I saw an envelope on the dining table. I opened it and there was $300.00 with a note.

It said: 'Dad! Just to tide you over. Your son will call you.'"

"Dick!" I said. "What do you think about this runaround?"

"Chandra! I should have given them the finger in the first place."

69

Doctor at any cost

My dad related this story to me when I visited my parents while on vacation from Sierra Leone where I was employed.

The parents of Nandakumar were fixated by an all- consuming desire that their son should become a doctor. From the time Nanda was a little kid they extolled the glamor of being a doctor. He could, they said to him, earn a lot of money, own a beautiful house, drive a posh car; and parents of pretty girls would fight tooth and nail to have him for their son-in-law. The parents knew that a son for a doctor would up their social status in the village.

"Nanda, the father would say, "I know it will cost a lot of money, which I do not have, but I will work long hours and save enough to send you to medical college." Nanda's father Appaiah was an Ayurvedic physician with a very modest practice.

I recall at this time there was only one medical college in Ceylon, and it was located in the capital, Colombo, far from the little village of Chankanai where Nanda's parents lived. Entering medical college was a Himalayan task.

Nanda's father was aware it was not going to be easy to achieve his obsessive ambition of seeing his son become a doctor. He put all his resources, physical and financial, into his dream of seeing his son qualify as a doctor.

Nanda was successful in obtaining admission to the medical college.

When the villagers learned that Appaiah's son had entered medical college and was on the threshold of becoming a doctor, their attitude toward this family changed. Wealthy parents of marriageable girls began visiting his house. At weddings and funerals, the parents were treated with a great deal of respect and prime seating was reserved for them. The parents lapped it all up to their heart's content.

For the first two years Nanda passed all his examinations. It was after that his troubles began. He got romantically involved with a Burgher (Biracial of Dutch descent) nurse and from then on, his studies went downhill and hit rock bottom. Nanda dropped out. His parents, however, were under the impression he was continuing his medical studies.

With the little knowledge of Ayurveda he had picked up observing the father and with the help of his nurse fiancé, the two of them began treating old dowagers who had hit hard times and extorting large sums of money. They also, my father said, got into the drug business. When the two of them realized the police were after them, they bolted to London and from there to Florida in the United States.

All the while the parents who were not English literate were under the impression he was specializing in medicine. The son saw to it they were well provided for. He, in fact, bought them a new car, the popular British Austin A-40, making this village a "one car town." The "old man" learned to drive, narrowly missing the palmyra and coconut trees on the narrow lanes, much to the titillation of the villagers. This was the first privately owned car in this little village. Most people either traveled by bus or by what they used to call a "hiring car" and what we call a taxi.

(*This is how the "hiring car" system worked. If your family had to attend, say, a wedding some distance away from your village, you would send word to the hiring car owner. He would turn up at the appointed time, take your family to the wedding, stay on until the wedding was over, and bring you back home for a pre- arranged fee. At the wedding he quite naturally would join in the fun and feast.*)

In Florida Nanda and his girlfriend were up to the same game, phony prescriptions and dealing in drugs. The police got wind of it, and an undercover agent exposed them. They were both arrested and were serving time when I heard the story from my father.

Before all this was reported in the newspapers in Ceylon and the news reached the village, the parents of Nandakumar on their way to a temple festival died in a car accident.

70

Open and Shut Case

It was claimed the doctor had made a wrong diagnosis and for that reason the child had died. The doctor was now being sued for a million dollars, and the lawyer for the deceased child's parents was confident that it was an open and shut case.

The doctor was given one month to produce his notes. During this period the doctor rewrote everything (this was a time before computers) validating his diagnosis. The notes were presented to the judge hearing the case. Everything appeared to be in order and there was no cause for worry.

The case attracted great interest locally and abroad. The lawyer for the parents was the popular Atul who had never lost a case. The more he studied the case, the plainer it was to him that he must lose a case at last--there was no getting around that painful fact. Even public sympathy was aroused on behalf of Atul. People said it was a pity to see him mar his career with a big prominent case like this, which certainly must go against him.

But after several restless nights an inspired idea flashed upon Atul, and he sprang out of bed delighted. He thought he'd got it.

At the final hearing the lawyer summoned a highly recognized professional printer and asked him when in his opinion the paper on which the doctor had made his notes had come out of the press. After very close examination and several calls the printer declared under six months.

The actual notes that the doctor made about the child's case were written over a period of three years.

71

Paternal Pride, Maternal Love

The father was a strict disciplinarian. He was a banker in a tiny village, the kind of village where no one stops, the kind of village people drive through heading somewhere else, the kind of village where everyone knows everyone else.

He was a veteran soldier of World War II who saw life as right or wrong, black or white--nothing in between, nothing gray. He brought to the office and to the home the culture of his army training, one of unquestionable obedience.

The mother was a homemaker to whom her two children, a son and daughter, were more precious than her two eyes.

The daughter was impeccable but the son, shifty.

Neighbors and friends, shop owners in the village as well, complained to the mother and daughter that the son was forever stealing something or other. The mother and daughter never once disclosed this to the father.

At the bank a petty clerk blabbered this to the father. The father was thoroughly humiliated.

The father came home and questioned the son and warned him that if all this was true, he could no longer stay in the house. "Either you leave or I go," the father warned.

The mother intervened. She said, "Not so fast. He's our son. He stays here. Don't you know this house belongs to me. This was my dad's wedding gift. If you leave, we will miss you but we'll manage. I'll settle our son's minor indiscretions as I have hitherto."

"Woman! You call these, minor; you'll regret this. Trust me."

So saying, the father walked out of the house for good.

The son did not change. He continued his bad ways, shielded by mother and daughter.

There was a break in at a nearby shop and substantial cash was stolen. The hidden camera showed that the son was the culprit. The son was sentenced to eight years in the clink.

On the day of sentencing mother and daughter were seated in the back row of the court.

When the sentence was delivered and the son was being led away, his mother screamed, "please, please don't take him away. He is a good boy."

The son turned around and addressed his mother:

"Ma! If only you had disciplined me when I was on to minor thefts, it wouldn't have come to this. You should have listened to dad. You spoiled me and now I am paying for it."

72

Valentine's Day

Tim and Terry have been going steady for three years. They liked to do something special on Valentine's Day.

On their first Valentine's Day they went to Puerto Vallarta in Mexico and had a grand time hitch-hiking, and they liked it.

On the second they climbed to Machu Picchu in Peru and thoroughly enjoyed it.

A few days before their third Valentine's Day Tim said to Terry, "Let's do something crazy this time."

They were now quite comfortable with each other. They felt anchored in the other's love. They were in a mood to do something wild.

"Sure," agreed Terry. "What will it be, Tim?"

"Let's go to a bar we have never been to before like "Pot and Belly." We'll go separately within, say, ten minutes of each other, sit separately, and make out with someone we have never met before. When it's time to leave you give me a sign, and we'll leave."

"That'll be fun, Tim," gushed Terry.

Tim and Terry entered "Pot and Belly," the bar they had never visited before. They walked in at separate times. Terry went over and sat next to a young man, ordered a drink, and started a conversation. Minutes later Tim entered and sat away from her, out of earshot. There was a vacant seat next to him.

A lady now walks in and sits next to Tim. Terry kept a close watch on Tim.

Tim was getting really flirtatious. Soon the pair was exchanging wisecracks and drinks were being consumed in rapid succession. They are now passing plates of steak to each other. Smiling radiantly, she was regaling him with stories, the light banter of people who are free and contented.

Terry began taking a closer look at this new girl Tim was talking to. There seemed to be a strange familiarity between them that she dismissed as wild imagination borne of mild jealousy. The other girl was in a tight sleeveless shirt that clung to her breasts and bared her midriff. Her skirt worn so-so showed off her thighs. Voluptuous! That's the only way you could describe her. Tim barely looked in the direction of Terry. She was making every effort to attract Tim's attention, but he didn't notice Terry and she had to keep on talking to the stranger.

The agreement was that when it was time to leave, they would give each other a sign. How could she give a sign when Tim was not even looking in her direction?

She then saw Tim get up from his seat and pull the woman's chair back for her to get out. And they both left. Through the window she could see Tim hail a taxi, the two of them boarded it and departed.

Terry went home alone and was up all night. Tim did not show up.

The next morning Terry went into the kitchen to make herself a cup of coffee, and there on the counter was a letter addressed to her.

Darling Terry:

Remember Vanessa whom I used to go out with. I have told you all about her--my high school heart throb. Three weeks ago, she came to my office, and we had a long chat. She went away to England thinking she could put our affair behind her and out of her mind but couldn't. She needs me. Her parents, who opposed our friendship thinking I was after their money, have passed away. Now that I have met her and she is here, I will not be able to put her out of my mind.

I am really sorry, and I know you will not be able to understand, but some day you will be able to forgive me. I expect to be married very soon. I love you as always. I realize now ours was only a boy and girl love.

I hope you have a great career. I know this for the best.

Please understand, Terry. You are a smart, pretty girl, Terry. I'm sure you'll find someone who truly deserves you.

Bye, Terry. Do keep in touch.

Lovingly,
Tim.

73

The Accident

The daughter was sixteen and had gotten her driving license, but her parents did not allow her to drive. "Not just yet" was their frustrating response to her pleas.

On this day the parents had gone out to a play and dinner thereafter. The daughter went over to a friend's house, and there was a party going on. At this party the daughter met a handsome football player, and they decided to go somewhere quiet.

The boy drove her to a well-known make-out spot. After being too friendly, the boy took out a bottle of Vodka and began drinking. Soon he was completely swished. The girl indicated it was time to get back to the party. The boy, of course, was in no condition to drive, and so the girl took the wheel with the boy now in the back seat fast asleep.

The girl, although in possession of a valid license, was a novice, and what was worse she had never driven at night.

She crashed head-on into an oncoming car.

At the hospital she was informed her friend in the back seat had died. Miraculously, she escaped with only minor bruises.

She inquired from the neighbors who had gathered outside whether they knew the whereabouts of her parents.

This is what she was told: "Some silly girl drove her car head-on into your parents' car, and they are both dead. The bodies can be seen in the morgue."

74

Strange Happenings

For the quite wild yet on the whole friendly narrative that I am about to relate, I neither expect nor solicit belief. Mad, indeed, would I be to expect it, where my very own senses defy their own evidence. Yet, mad I am not. Believe me--I dream not. It's beyond my intellectual breadth and depth to establish a sequence of cause and effect. I won't even try.

Save in supplication do I present these lines.

When Horatio, having seen the ghost of Hamlet's father, the king, on a gun platform atop the battlements of castle Elsinore and having reported it to his friend with bemused skepticism, Hamlet's response was:

"There are more things in heaven and earth, Horatio, than are dreamt of in your philosophy."

Lucas and Merrilos were very close friends. They went to the same high school, played cricket and soccer for the university contemporaneously in a little island in the Indian Ocean called Ceylon, and now they find themselves settled down in Stamford, Connecticut. Merrilos and Lucas worked for an international organization.

Lucas and Merrilos could walk into the other's home without advance notice, open the refrigerator, pick up a beer, and sit down for what they would call a "con chat." Shoot the breeze. That close they were. They were both married and had children.

One day after a swim, while sipping beer, they agreed that when one of them died, the dead should contact the living.

It was evening. Merrilos and wife Maxios were about to leave for a dinner party. Merrilos, an exercise freak, said to his wife that he would quickly do a run along the main road and get back. He never returned. He was run over by a city bus.

After the memorial service Lucas and wife brought Maxios back home and were about to leave when Maxios suggested the couple stay and have dinner. The couple politely declined the kind offer, not wanting to add to her chores.

"No, please stay on and have dinner with me," Maxios pleaded to a disinclined Lucas and his wife.

Then it happened.

There was no smoke and yet the fire alarm went off. A pan on the stove fell off and spilled water all over the kitchen floor. A packet of beans on the kitchen table burst. They heard a car come up the driveway, and they all anxiously looked out of the window thinking some friends were visiting but there were none to be seen.

Lucas and his wife, completely shaken up by what they heard and saw, said to Maxios:

"We'll have dinner with you; and if you think it will help, we'll spend the night here."

With these words the strange happenings ceased.

Maxios and Merrilos were a devoted couple. Maxios could not be consoled. Every day she went to Merrilos' grave and sat there for hours. She claimed Merrilos communicated with her.

A few years went by and one day Maxios was introduced to a stranger at the church. He was rich, handsome, and pursued her with a passion she had never known before. The wealthy stranger asked Maxios to marry him. Maxios was confused and did not know what to say. She asked for time to consider the proposal.

That night Maxios went to Merrilos' grave. She sat on the bench opposite the headstone.

"There's a newcomer in town who wants to marry me. He appears to love me very much. But I don't know what I should do. I am still so sad I lost you. Please tell me what I should tell him." This continued for one more day and on the third day Maxios prayed, "Merrilos! I need to give an answer today. I need to know." "Please, please," she begged.

She felt a tingle in her hands and arms; and when she breathed, something light and sad enveloped her.

When she looked up, she saw a lady and a child pass by. The child broke loose from his mother, came up to Maxios, and crying said, "NO – NO – NO!"

When Maxios looked up again, the mother and child were nowhere to be seen.

It came to light the ardent suitor had three wives, all wealthy widows, in three different states. The police were watching him closely.

75

Unruffled

During a ten- day visit to Nicaragua she had a steamy affair with a man. They were both Zoroastrians while her husband is a Buddhist.

On her return to Connecticut it takes her one whole week before she comes clean about the affair to her husband. She awaits his reaction. There is none.

"Aren't you curious?" she asks.

He says, "Hell no!"

"I'm very upset you don't seem to care," she says.

"Do you want me to be the kind of man who becomes upset so easily?"

"Did you say so easily? Good God, man, here I am returning after a fling with a total stranger for a whole week and your muscles do not even twitch. Do you realize we both had a lot in common, belonging to the same faith? Does it not strike you that I could have stayed on?"

He is unmoved.

"You are back, aren't you?" he says and goes about his work.

When she sees him calmly going about his work, she realizes this is the way he is getting back at her.

"SHIT!" she swears and makes a dash to the kitchen. He hears the din of clanking cups and broken bowls and more swearing.

76

Still Waters Run Deep

I have met this gentleman very briefly a couple of times. Once at lunch on a Sunday at a Sri Lankan friend's house in Mamba Point. Thereafter a couple of times at the swimming club. Very reserved, polite and polished in his demeanor and conversation. The kind of man who will not go out of his way to make friends. I understood he was American, now living in Monrovia, Liberia (West Africa) where I was employed. Not much was known about him. When I inquired about him, our friend Maha said he met him at the club and, since he was single, had invited him to lunch. He was called Jimmy something or other. This happened in the mid-seventies.

Liberia is very kind to Americans. Even if an American should over stay his visa, he is not harassed as other visitors would. Most Liberians received their advanced education and professional training in New York and are very proud of it. They are referred to as "Americos."

Jimmy was attracted to a pretty Liberian teller and would take every opportunity to visit the bank and make conversation with her. The attraction was mutual I would presume.

One such day when he was at the bank, he heard screams from women and quickly rushed to the place from where the screams were issuing.

Unnoticed by the mother and a friend who were at the bank to transact business, a ten year-old girl, June, in a spirit of mischievous play, leaving her older sister Louise outside, stepped into the vault and shut it. She had then shot the bolts and turned the knobs of the combination as she had seen the manager, Duncan, do many times before.

Mr. Duncan, the elderly banker, seeing this rushed to the vault and vigorously tugged at the handle.

"Lord!" He screamed. The door cannot be opened. The clock hasn't been wound nor has the combination set."

Louise's mother screamed hysterically.

Mr. Duncan was now trembling. Raising his shaking hand and his voice, he very loudly said, "All be quiet for a moment." Addressing June, he said., "Listen to me carefully."

A ghostly silence followed. A crowd of customers and staff had by now gathered outside the vault. They all could hear the faint sound of the child wildly shrieking in terror in the dark silent vault.

"My precious darling!" wailed the mother. "She will die of fright! Open the door please! Oh, break it open! Can't you men do something?"

"There isn't a man nearer than a hundred miles away who can open that door. We have to get in touch with the suppliers of the vault," said Duncan in a shaky voice.

"My God! What shall we do? That child – she can't stand it long in there. There isn't enough air. She will soon go into convulsions from fright."

The mother, frantic by now, began beating the door with her bare fists.

Someone in the gathering suggested they blow it up with dynamite. There was no shortage of zany suggestions.

All this was unfolding while Maha's friend Jimmy was watching wistfully with detached curiosity, standing apart from the crowd. The Liberian teller Kusimi now approached Jimmy and asked coyly "Can't you do something, please?" He looked at her admiringly, realizing this was a God-given opportunity to show off and said, "Anything to please you, girl."

So saying, he walked out to his car, collected his bag, which was his closest companion at all times, and came to the vault.

He threw off his coat, pulled up his shirt sleeves, tightened his belt, placed the bag on a nearby counter, and opened it. He laid out the shining, queer looking implements swiftly and orderly while humming "Sweet By and By" in a low tone, impervious to his surroundings, while the crowd of onlookers in fearful silence watched him as if under a spell.

"Get away from that door all of you," he ordered.

In a minute Jimmy's pet drill was biting smoothly into the steel door. In ten minutes--breaking his own burglarious record--he threw back the bolts and opened the door.

June, had passed out, but safe, was gathered into her mother's arms.

Jimmy, put on his coat; and, humming "Hakuna Matata, no worries for the rest of my days," he walked outside the railings toward the front door.

Jimmy was a yegg with an enormous reputation, the chief architect of many successful bank robberies in Chicago and elsewhere. After the last big haul, he decamped to Liberia with the intention of marrying a Liberian to avoid extradition.

The last I heard, Jimmy was married to Kusimi and they are happily settled in Monrovia.

77

"Where were You?"

My wife tells me she would like to visit her office buddy who has been admitted to the hospital after an automobile accident and asks whether I would accompany her. I say to her "no problem," so long as I take a book with me and there is a bathroom within sniffing distance.

And so, we set out.

On arrival I see a canteen in the foyer. Thoughts of a nice cup of coffee sizzle in my head. I say to my wife, "You go ahead, I'll stay here." "No," my wife says. "I' d rather you come along (10th floor); you can do your reading there."

I do a courtesy bow to the patient and retire to what appears to be a small dining room with my book. There are about four visitors, all for the same patient, who is an elderly gentleman. More visitors come along for the same patient. They are all in a happy chatty mood.

I take a seat away from them under the window with my back against the wall. I begin my reading.

Two hours later. "It's about time," I tell myself (by now far too rested). There are more errands before the day is done.

I step out of the room.

"Where were you?" asks a nurse, looking straight into my, by now weary, teary eyes.

"What do you mean?" I counter question her. "This is where I have been all this while, and this is where my wife wanted me to wait for her. Just like the 'boy who stood on the burning deck.' Do you know the story?"

"No," she says, appearing to want to hear it.

"Many, many, many years ago the English naval squadron under the one-eyed Lord Nelson sailed in. They had caught the French fleet at anchor unprepared. The French ship was called, I think, L'Orient. It soon found itself flanked by English ships attacking from both sides. The English set the L'Oreient ablaze.

"It was then the English saw an amazing sight. There on 'the burning deck' they saw a boy standing alone. Not like me seated reading a book. His name was Casabianca. He was the son of one of the French officers.

"What's happening to the elevator. It's not coming up.

"Anyway, his father, an officer, told his son, Casabianca, who was just twelve years, mind you, 'stand right here, don't leave the post, I'll soon be back.' So saying, he left. And there the boy stood just as his father had asked him to. Just as I was told by my wife to remain in the room.

"The L'Orient was set ablaze, the fire reached the powder magazine deep down in the hold. The boy perished when the ship erupted in a massive explosion."

As the nurse and I stepped out of the elevator, there was a cop waiting. "Where were you? We have been looking for you, sir" he says to me, not amused.

My wife from the far end comes running. "Where were you? We looked all over for you. All ten floors. The Emergency Room. Every bathroom. Where were you?"

78

My Friendly Neighbor

They were my neighbors. When I came to know them, it was a family of a mother, who was a widow, six sons, and three daughters. Did I say, yes, and a dog, too. All lived in a townhouse with two and a half bed rooms and shower upstairs, sitting room, kitchen, dining room and one toilet on the ground floor. So many humans and a dog in so little real estate. A miracle in economy.

One could not expect to find a better family. The children loved their mother, and in return the mother adored her children. Never have I heard a harsh word emanate from this house, a family living in such physical and emotional proximity. Devout Christians who never imposed their faith on others by doing anything like handing out pamphlets. (It is not uncommon, when you answer the door bell, to be handed "Jesus Loves You" literature by well-meaning folks.)

They lived very simply.

Just a word about the dog and my friend, the youngest son. In the evenings he would take the dog for a walk. No, it was the other way around--the dog would take him for a walk. He holds the leash and follows the dog to wherever the dog may take him. "It's his walk," he would say to us.

There were times when my parents would be out of town, and this wonderful mother would insist I have my meals with them. The meals were simple but served with love and affection. What you see is what there is. Many a day I got up from the table mildly hungry. I cannot overstate it. The mother was a kind lady. I liked them. The youngest son, the dog walker, and I attended the same high school.

"We are all men, in our own natures frail, and capable of our flesh, few are angels." Shakespeare in Henry VIII

One of the sons, much senior to me, was addicted to that "No Winner" game--betting on the horses. The mother would plead with this son to kick the habit, and he would say, "Don't worry, Ma. I am going to win big and then we'll all be fine." Until one day he won some money. This was the day he was going to treat his mother. He took time off from work, bought all the things his mother liked, loaded them onto his motor cycle, and set out for home. On his way he passed a restaurant. "Aha," he says to himself. "Let me get some of the kinds of food Ma likes." He runs into the restaurant, stands in line, and gets the food his mother would like.

He gets back to find, "gone." Every bit of it.

79

Nipped in the Bud

The mother came to the United States as a visitor when she was eighteen with an aunt. A few days before her visitor's visa expired she bolted from home. She dreaded going back to her village in Nicaragua. Because she didn't have proper papers, she took on any job she could find. Wealthy homes hired her as a nanny. Super markets to clean toilets. Male employers, aware of her illegal status, raped and abused her. She was too scared to go to the police. The mother conceived as a result of a rape. Her daughter had a ringside view of the torment and hardship her mother suffered. She could not go to school. She followed her mother wherever she worked and helped her.

When she turned eighteen, the girl's mother died; however, the girl's misery continued. She begged for change on the streets, and like her mother sold her body for sustenance, and like her mother she conceived as the result of a rape.

She gave birth to an extremely beautiful baby girl. At birth the baby did not cry, instead she giggled. Her mother strangled her.

80

"The grass is always greener..."

Selvam was the store's manager, and I was its accountant. Selvam's sister, a nurse, was married to Williams, a sales representative. To be a successful salesman one must have a knack for it--the proper temperament, the ability with a smile to take "NO" for an answer. Salesmen rely mainly on commissions. Williams was a traveling salesman who was away from home for long periods. Salesmen have to make calls at various companies out of state, remain patiently in waiting rooms, sometimes for hours. And at the end of it he may not get an order. As I have said, Williams just did not have what it took to be a good salesman.

At this time there was a demand for nurses in the United Kingdom so Williams and wife Lorraine decided to migrate to the United Kingdom. With the the paltry sum of money they had and with a little bit of help from Selvam they arrived in the United Kingdom.

Lorraine, being a nurse, got a job right away. One problem, though, was that Lorraine was put on night duty all week, every week. She had no choice but to take the job.

Williams had tremendous difficulty finding a job. After many frustrating tries he found a job with London Transport. He had to report to the railway station at seven o'clock sharp. If he was late the train would leave with a substitute, and he wouldn't be paid, which was something the new arrivals could not afford.

Williams and his wife never had any time together. When one was at home, the other was at work. The only time they saw the other was on the road near the house when passing, Williams hurrying to catch the bus to the railway station and Lorraine returning from the hospital. They communicated by notes left on the dining room table. Should one forget to put down something on the note, it would be shouted out loud when passing on the street—things like "Your breakfast is in the oven" or "There's a very important letter from home. Read it."

Strange. I see Williams in my office in Sri Lanka. "What on earth are you doing here?" I ask him. "We couldn't take it anymore. So, we're back," he tells me.

Six months later.

In connection with some work, Selvam comes to my office, and I ask him: "By the way, how are Williams and your sister faring?" And he replies, "They have returned to the U.K. They could not get a job here. Lucky for them their old employers were willing to take them back."

Which reminds me to relate my next story.

81

Three in One

handra Singh, Chitra Singh and Siva Singh arrived at Heathrow Airport independently. At the airport they talked. They became friends, united by a common destiny. They found that all three of them had been assured by a mutual friend they could each have a low paying job in a soda bottling factory that was in operation twenty-four hours a day. As I have said, the pay was very small and they carried very little money with them.

They needed a place to stay. How did they solve this problem? Leave it to the ingenuity of the Singhs, I say.

They right-away bought a newspaper and scanned the wanted columns. One, which fortuitously was close to the factory, read "Wanted tenant. Single room with a bed and a bath and toilet attached. Rent twenty pounds sterling payable in advance weekly."

The three turned up at the landlady's house, and said they would take it. The three Singhs told the landlady each of them would pay a third of the rental. She need have no worry. The rent every week will be paid in full, they individually and collectively assured her.

The landlady was puzzled beyond words. "You look like decent folks. I have only one room to rent. How will you all manage in one room?"

"Have no worries. We have a plan," they assured her.

The next morning the three Singhs met the manager of the factory and requested they be put on three separate shifts of eight hours each.

Each of the Singhs, by juggling his working and waking hours, was able to get eight hours of sleep. They carried on like this for several months until each of them married a local girl and moved out.

When I interviewed the landlady, an elderly widow, she was all praise for the three Singhs. "Those children were so very nice to me. They were of great help. I miss them."

"Did they pay the rent on time?" I asked. "Always and on time," she confirmed.

82

In Pursuit of Perfection

"No one is perfect"

How many times have we heard this? The child to father, student to teacher.

Homo sapiens have been forever in pursuit of a perfection that continues to elude them. They try to find it in painting as in Da Vinci's "Mona Lisa," in Michelangelo's "Creation of Adam" and in the other inspired paintings on the ceiling of the Sistine Chapel. In music Bach and Beethoven strove for perfection. In sculpture we have the almost "perfect" statue of David in Florence. The Greeks strained hard to slake their thirst for perfection through mythology--Adonis, Aphrodite, Achilles and the rest of the panoply.

The Hindus went even further. Perfection was manifested in the form of deities. For learning, the Goddess Saraswathi; for wealth, the Goddess Lakshmi; for love, Sri Krishna. who was believed to be the eighth avatar of Lord Vishnu. Even birth, preservation, death, and destruction took godly forms before which believers genuflect in awe.

The fifth Moghul emperor Shah Jahan wanted a perfect tribute to the memory of his favorite wife, Mumtaz Mahal, and so ordered the construction of a mausoleum to match her beauty--and so the Taj Mahal came into being.

Over the years Jesus received a makeover in this pursuit of perfection. The Middle Eastern Jew who traveled on foot and fasted for long periods is now presented to the world with blue eyes, flowing blond hair, and broad shoulders. The great Gnostic master Valentinus went so far as to say that Jesus "ate and drank but did not defecate." His loss of cool in the temple when he turned the tables on the money changers is not uncontrolled temper but "righteous indignation." His mother was a virgin; Mary's own birth was free of original sin, an immaculate conception.

And before that Job was the perfect one. God challenged Satan to break the moral spine of Job. And Satan threw everything including the kitchen sink at him. It is reported Job did not budge. Think about it. With God having put his money on Job, what chance in hell had Satan?

This may be part of the reason why Islam sternly forbids the pictorial proliferation of the prophet Mohammed and why idol worship is anathema. The believer is free to picture the prophet in the manner he is comfortable with.

A cardinal is human one day, runs for office, and becomes the infallible pope the next day. His pronouncements carry the imprimatur of a papal bull. All too perfect, all too soon.

The kings and queens of England become kings and queens not by the prosaic path of mundane succession, sometimes even skewed by the rightful heir marrying a divorcee, but by "Divine Right," and thus they bestow on themselves the aura of divinity. The Queen of England cannot be brought to court because of the legal maxim that "The Queen can do no wrong" is sacrosanct.

The Japanese Emperor derives his authority from the sun. The former North Korean dictator Kim IL Sung, who committed harrowing atrocities, was "God," and that makes his son, the current dictator, "The Son of God."

If we are to accept the biblical version of the origin of life, the first man and woman ceased to be perfect with the fall from grace in the Garden of Eden.

Nothing perfect can emerge from things imperfect.

If we are to accept Darwin's theory of evolution, then man is continuing to evolve, adapting to changing conditions – technology, environment, moral standards and so on. What appeared perfect one day is made obsolete by subsequent events, innovations and inventions.

An extract from Robert Penn Warren's great novel, <u>All the King's Men</u>, is worth noting. When the protagonist, Jack Burden, is ordered by corrupt William Clark to get some dirt on the "upright judge," Burden replies that there can't possibly be something on such an honorable man. "There's always something," Willie replies. "Man is conceived in sin and born in corruption and he passeth from the stink of the didie to the stench of the shroud, there's always something." Willie Clark proves right. There's something on the "upright judge" and tragedy results.

In <u>Cider House Rules</u> Dr.Larch, the director of the orphanage, is so dedicated to the kids one would think he is a saint, but then we discover to our disappointment he isn't.

Noted author Ayn Rand in her well- known novel, <u>The Fountainhead</u>, postulates, "I want to present the perfect man and his perfect life" and for this purpose selects for her hero Howard Roark. This becomes her magnificent obsession.

At the 2008 Summer Olympics held in Beijing, China, we saw "pigtailed and smiling," Lin, age nine, performing "Ode to the Motherland." In actual fact the voice was that of another girl, Yang, who was judged the best singer. Why then was she not allowed to perform? She was not cute enough. The authorities believed, "The child on camera should be flawless in image, internal feeling, and expression." Since they could not find all the attributes to project a perfect image in one person, they had to resort to a "cut and paste" job of two kids.

Who knows, in years to come Mother Theresa, who with bent back and unbroken spirit served humanity wallowing knee-deep in the filth and squalor of Calcutta, may hang on the drawing room walls of affluent homes looking like Marilyn Monroe. Of course, she won't be singing "Happy Birthday, Mister President."

Homo sapiens will continue to "look before and after and pine for what is not; our sweetest songs are those that tell us of our saddest thoughts"

END OF STORY

Many thanks to you, intrepid, gentle reader, for giving me a chance to present the fruits of my labor, the product of one who is self-taught and whose only justification for burdening you with these "Itty Bitty Tiny Tall" tales is that he just cannot help himself. He must read and he must write. If these tiny tall ones made you smile just once, he will consider himself handsomely rewarded.

"Whether we shall meet again, I know not; if we do meet again, why, we shall smile.

If not, why then this parting was well made." - William Shakespeare.
I believe:
"There's a divinity that shapes our ends." - William Shakespeare.
Why bother?

PICTURES OF THE LAKE DISTRICT
- HOME OF THE ENGLISH POETS
- WORDSWORTH, COLERIDGE
AND CHARLES LAMB

Printed in the United States
By Bookmasters